Traded

LISA SUZANNE

TRADED
VEGAS ACES: THE QUARTERBACK
BOOK ONE

Published in the United States of America by Books by LS, LLC.

ISBN: 9798450058672

Cover Designed by Najla Qamber Designs
Editing by It's Your Story Content Editing

VEGAS ACES

THE QUARTERBACK

Traded

BOOKS BY LISA SUZANNE

VEGAS ACES
Home Game (Book One)
Long Game (Book Two)
Fair Game (Book Three)
Waiting Game (Book Four)
End Game (Book Five)

VEGAS ACES: THE QUARTERBACK
Traded (Book One)
Tackled (Book Two)
Timeout (Book Three)
Turnover (Book Four)
Touchdown (Book Five)

A LITTLE LIKE DESTINY SERIES
A Little Like Destiny (Book One)
Only Ever You (Book Two)
Clean Break (Book Three)

MY FAVORITE BAND STANDALONES
Take My Heart
The Benefits of Bad Decisions
Waking Up Married
Driving Me Crazy
It's Only Temporary
The Replacement War

Visit Lisa on Amazon for more titles

DEDICATION

As always, to my 3M.

And also to Hot Luke and Sexy Ellie (and all you who fell in love with them) for starting this whole thing. I can't wait to keep visiting you in future books. Xoxo

CHAPTER 1

"What if Jack Dalton actually shows up?" I squeal to Shannon as we both stare out the window at the flashing lights that pass by us in a blur. "You *know* he's number one on my hot list."

She laughs. "If he does show up and spots you in that cat burglar costume, you will definitely catch his attention. Or any one of the other dozen celebrities rumored to be making an appearance tonight."

I laugh. "Yeah, the hot quarterback of the Broncos will pick *me* out of every other woman in the club. There's not a chance in hell he's choosing the cat burglar over the richer, more famous, probably sluttier kittens dancing Halloween night away."

"You never know. Did you ever think you'd be attending a party like this?"

I shake my head.

"See? So you never know what could happen."

Shannon won tickets on the radio to this Halloween party at some fancy club at some fancy hotel on the Las Vegas Strip. It's a party neither of us would ever have be able to afford on our own, but tonight, our entire tab is paid for. All we have to do is show up and have a good time with the rich and famous.

I slip my mask off as we walk through the casino, and then I put it firmly back into place once we get in line to enter the club. She gives her last name to the bouncer, and voila. We're in.

We beeline for the bar, and she hands over the confirmation for our tab. She settles into some rum special, and I pull out the big guns with Fireball on the rocks.

If I'm going to let go and have a good time tonight and even think of the possibility of getting a hot stud up in this kitty, then I'm going to arm myself with the most potent of all my favorite drinks. I've been working nonstop lately, and I haven't had a night off in a long, long time. So I'm partying it up old school style tonight.

With liquor in hand, we head to the dance floor. I glance around, and just like every club I've ever danced in, there's a mix of couples grinding and singles looking around—but tonight, everybody's in a costume. It's sort of hard to tell who's just a regular Joe and who might be a celebrity.

I like having the cat mask on as I look around in the dark room with flashing lights as we all move to the familiar songs. It makes me feel like I can be somebody I'm not, and as I empty my first drink, I'm starting to feel the familiar fuel of liquid confidence.

Shannon and I each grab a second drink, and the crush of people that've shown up since we first got here makes it a little harder to find an open spot on the dance floor.

It's as I'm nearing the bottom of my second drink, already hot and starting to sweat in my costume from the heat of bodies moving all around me, that it seems as though everyone in our vicinity swings their heads toward the door at the same time.

I look in that direction, too, but I can't see over the people in front of me. "What's going on?" I ask Shannon, and she glances at me and shrugs. She gets up onto her tiptoes but can't see over the crowd, either.

"That's Jack Dalton!" someone beside me yells over the music.

"Jack Dalton?" someone else yells back. "Jack Dalton!"

I was raised in a household where we spent Sundays watching football. I know who Jack Dalton is. Who doesn't? Who hasn't stared with dreamy eyes at the television on Sunday afternoons as they watch him catch the ball the center hikes before he drops back into the pocket with discipline and confidence as he looks down the field for an open receiver?

Hot.

Like...*super* hot.

And we're at the same nightclub. At least I *think* we are. That's what some-drunk-body said beside me a second ago.

Can you even imagine being at the same place as someone like Jack Dalton? What if we bump into each other at the bar and he's super into cat burglars and he sweeps me up into his arms to take me away?

Yeah, because that's my luck.

If anything, I have the complete *opposite* luck when it comes to the male species. Instead of sweeping me into their arms, I tend to get pushed down and trampled.

I step up onto my tiptoes to try to get a better look, and that's when I spot a tall, athletic man flanked by two burly men. He has this demeanor about him that makes everyone in this place stop to look. It's extreme confidence mixed with some strange sort of control, like he has this authority over the club and everyone in it. And I suppose he does. He's one of the most famous football players in the world. He's a gazillionaire and he's talented and he's freaking *gorgeous.*

If I thought he was hot on my television on Sundays, well, he's even more of a treat in the flesh even from across a dark room. He's tall, and he just has this big presence about him that takes over this place. He moves through the club with an easy smile, and a small entourage follows closely behind him.

"Holy cheeseballs," I murmur. "It really is Jack Dalton."

I turn and look at Shannon, and she grabs me by the biceps.

"It's Jack Dalton!" we both squeal at the same time.

So maybe we're a tad tipsy already.

"We have to meet him," she says. She grabs my arm and starts pulling me in his direction. "We have to get you a shot with him."

"Oh my God, Shan. You're freaking delusional." I can't deny it—I like where her head's at, but this just isn't realistic. Not only is he flanked by club security plus his own entourage, but he can have any woman in this place...in the *world.*

Is he even single? I could swear I read that someone's knocked up with his kid, but maybe that was somebody else. I'm not some crazy stalker who knows every detail about his life just because I find him attractive.

"Okay, if you don't want him, he can be *my* hook-up!" Shannon squeals.

My brows dip as my claws emerge and I don't even know why my claws are coming out at this entirely unrealistic conversation.

"You're getting married next year," I not so gently remind her.

She wrinkles her nose. "Oh, right. That."

I giggle.

"We just need to get his attention." She looks around, and then she snaps her finger in a dramatic *aha! I've got it!* type of thing. "We'll get you in his path and he can swoop in and save you and then you can work your magic."

"What do you mean *swoop in and save me*?" I ask, narrowing my eyes at her.

"Just follow me and play along," she says, and she moves quickly. I struggle to keep up with her in these hooker boots. I never wear heels, but these came with the costume. They're four-inch platform things and my feet are freaking killing me, but the Fireball is helping to numb the pain.

One more and everything will start to numb. My tolerance is pretty low these days since my job occupies me pretty much twenty-four-seven and this is my first outing in months.

I'm concentrating so hard on not tripping in these stupid shoes that I don't even see Shannon coming when she plows into me. I tumble to the ground with a shriek and a curse. When I land on the floor, my knee screams in pain and I'm positive I've broken both ankles and definitely bumped my knee on the sticky concrete floor. My glass goes flying out of my hands and shatters a few feet away, and as my hand slams to the floor, a little shard cuts into the side of my palm.

I'm about to scream out *what the fuck* to Shannon when the most incredible thing happens.

A deep voice is so close to my ear that the heat sends a shiver through my entire core. "Jesus Christ, are you okay?"

I turn to look up at the source of that sexy voice and find myself face-to-face with Mr. Jack Motherfucking Dalton. My eyes widen as they gaze up into his intense, navy blue ones, and I'm rendered temporarily speechless. My cheeks burn—not that he can see them in the dark or under this mask—and my thighs clench together as I get a whiff of his scent.

Oh my God.

His scent.

He smells like a fucking dream. I want to breathe him in and only smell Jack Dalton for the rest of eternity.

Holy shit.

Did Shannon's ridiculous plan actually work?

"What the hell happened?" he asks. He picks up my hand in his, and that's when I see the blood. It's not a lot, but the glass definitely sliced my hand. "You're bleeding," he murmurs, his voice husky and dripping with sex.

I force out words. "I'm okay." *My friend pushed me so I'd fall in front of you* sounds ridiculous, so I cut it off there.

He holds the back of my bleeding hand in his as he runs the fingertips of his other hand tenderly along my boot and toward my knee. Shivers shoot up on my body at every spot he touches. "Looks like you banged up your knee pretty good." He turns around and looks at his entourage. "Danny!" He flicks his neck as if to tell Danny to come over, and another attractive man kneels down beside us. "Can you check her knee?"

Danny nods. "Let's get her up to your suite for some privacy."

"I'm okay," I protest, but why the *fuck* am I protesting when I should definitely just let this happen?

Jack nods, and then, and I'm not lying, I swear to God this actually happens, he literally sweeps me up off the floor and into his arms.

He carries me through the club, and if my knee is freaking *broken* it'll be worth it just to have this memory. And if I wasn't two Fireballs deep, I'd never have the nerve to wrap my arms around his neck as he carries me, and then I never would've gotten the chance to breathe him in and allow that woodsy, masculine scent to permanently stamp onto my consciousness.

I will never forget this moment as long as I live.

I'll never forget the butterflies swimming around in my stomach or the buzzing in my head or the clenching of my thighs.

When Shannon asked me to go with her to this little Halloween shindig she won tickets to, in my wildest dreams I never could've imagined that I'd be on my way to Jack Dalton's private suite as he carries me through the club in his arms.

Yet here I am, and I have all my fingers and toes crossed that this is going to lead to so much more than just him checking out my knee to make sure it isn't broken.

CHAPTER 2

Jack follows some hostess at the club toward a set of stairs, and he carries me up them. The hostess glances back at me with disdain, and I'm not sure if it's because I'm bleeding or if it's because she's jealous Jack is showering me with this attention.

Shannon's wide eyes meet mine as she sneaks a glance over at me, and I almost laugh at the look on her face. She wants to apologize, but she also wants me to thank her. I'm torn between being mad and being grateful. I guess I'll feel a certain way once I know the extent of the damage...and also probably once the Fireball wears off.

He carries me along a small hallway before coming to a stop at a one of the suites. It's separated from the other rooms with walls for privacy and double doors that are currently open to the balcony that overlooks the partiers down below. It's quite a view, but I can't seem to stop looking at the hero who just carried me through the club.

He lies me down across one of the couches inside the suite and kneels on the floor beside me.

"What are you drinking?" he asks, his eyes level with mine.

"Fireball." My voice comes out all husky and low.

He gives me a look I can't decode, but then he says to the hostess, "A Fireball for the girl, and I'll take a gin and tonic, heavy on the gin."

She nods and disappears, and for a second it's just the two of us. I don't know where Shannon or the rest of his entourage went, and I'm about to ask when the man he called Danny walks in and shuts the double doors. It's immediately quiet in here despite the loud music and pulse of the bass just on the other side of the door. Danny flicks on a light, and I squint beneath my cat mask in the brightness of the room.

"Where did my friend go?" I ask.

"She's hanging out with my buddies," Jack says. He stays close beside me.

Danny hands him a cloth then bends down to take a look at my knee, and Jack takes my hand tenderly in his. As Danny pokes and inspects my knee, Jack gently works on cleaning around the cut on my hand. I watch him carefully, and I wince a little as he runs the cloth over my wound.

His hands are huge. What is it about hands that makes them so damn sexy? I think for just a beat about what his hands do. It's not just the talent he has with throwing footballs. The gossip sites report on his penchant for pleasure and his way with women. He's been with actresses and singers, sports reporters and porn stars, and everyone in between. What I *don't* typically hear about is when he hooks up with cat burglars at nightclubs on Halloween...but that doesn't mean we can't make some new headlines.

I refocus my attention on his lean, strong hands. His fingers are long, and all I can think about for a second is those fingers touching my body everywhere. A wild ache presses between my thighs.

"Let's get the boot off so I can get a better look," Danny says.

I sit up to unzip, but Jack beats me to it. He pulls the zipper down, down, down, and each hiss of the teeth unfastening pulses another beat of need through my chest.

He slips off my boot, and he palms my calf, and Jesus I feel like I could just lean back and close my eyes and fall into the throes of pleasure.

"Does your ankle feel okay?" Jack asks as he pulls my foot into his hand and moves it back and forth a little.

I'm snapped back to reality. "Yeah, it feels okay." He slips my other boot off, too, and does the same thing to my foot, and while both ankles are a little sore from the boots, I think I'm going to live.

"I think the boots saved you," he says, and his eyes travel up toward mine. God, he's intense. My chest zips with nerves as thrills dart up my spine.

Danny prods at my knee. "You banged it up pretty good, but the good news is I don't see any swelling. I'd recommend resting it a few days, but you should be fine."

"Thank you," I say softly.

He nods and moves to leave, and does this mean I'm going to be alone with Jack?

I don't know this guy even though I *feel* like I do. That's sort of the problem with celebrities, isn't it? We all feel like we know them personally since we see them doing their thing on the screen, or, in Jack's case, in person if we're lucky enough to grab tickets to a game.

But we don't know them. Not really.

We just know what they let us see when they post little peeks of their lives on social media, or we know them by what the media publishes about them, which might be true and might not be.

Yet I feel this intrinsic connection with this man, like I know a little something about him. He established an immediate trust between us when he scooped me up and took care of my injuries, minor as they turned out to be.

And now...what?

We screw here in this private suite?

Danny flicks off the light and shuts the door behind him when he leaves the two of us alone in this big suite. I don't owe anybody anything, and certainly not my body...and yet I find myself wanting to hand it over to Jack to do whatever he wants with it.

This is *Jack Dalton.*

When will I get the chance at something like this ever again in my life?

Shannon said I needed a night of fun, and this is the direction I want to take it.

"So why a cat burglar?" he asks. He's still on the floor beside me.

I laugh. The truth of the matter is that it was in the bargain bin after Halloween last year and I held onto it to wear this year.

I didn't think I'd be wearing it in a private suite at a club with a celebrity when I picked it up. The reality hasn't quite hit me just yet.

"Long story. Why no costume?" I ask.

He shrugs. "I don't really do the costume thing."

"You're playing the Aces on Sunday, aren't you?"

He nods. "You know who I am?" he asks carefully.

I make some sort of weird *pfft* sound. "Of course. Doesn't everybody?"

A knock at the door causes him to pause, and he gets up to answer it. I stay perched in my spot on the couch. He returns a moment later with our drinks, and I note that he closed the door behind the waitress. Do we still need privacy? What's he even doing here? He has a game in two days. Isn't he supposed to be somewhere?

"What are you doing here?" I finally blurt as he hands me my glass of Fireball.

He chuckles. "Paid appearance. I take pictures with some key people and bow out." He sets his drink on the end table and picks up my legs. He sits on the couch then settles my legs onto his lap, and he's so damn casual about it all like we've known each other for ages...but we haven't. It's barely been minutes.

"Have you taken your pictures?" I ask.

He shakes his head. "I'll get to it. I just got here when—" he cuts himself off.

"When I tripped and fell in front of you?" I supply, and he laughs.

"I was going to say when a beautiful kitty cat stumbled across my path."

I giggle and take a sip of my drink for a little added liquid courage. He strokes my legs absently, and his eyes move to mine at my giggle. His are serious. Intense.

My giggling ceases immediately as this new sort of tension swirls around us. Is this just *him* creating this atmosphere? Is he like this with every woman, or is there actually something between us?

I take one more bolstering sip—a gulp, really—and I set my glass on the table beside the couch. And then I make my move.

I sit up and sort of crawl over to him, and I swing one leg over to straddle his lap. My dress hikes up so my panties rub against his jeans, and the rough friction there is nearly too much. I don't even feel the pain in my knee when I'm this close to him. "You think I'm beautiful?" I ask shyly, my voice a contrast to my not-so-shy actions of straddling him.

He lets out a low chuckle. "What I can see of you, yeah. A gorgeous, sweet little body. Long, wavy, dark hair...exactly my type. Your eyes may be hidden beneath that mask, but they're beyond expressive. Even in the darkness of this club, I can tell their exact hazel shade. Too light to be brown, too dark to be green. And the way they've been flashing at me since the moment we met is driving me crazy."

He shifts his hips under me, and need pulses down low in my belly as I feel his erection beneath me. I shift my hips over his and nearly let out a moan at how good he feels.

"You've got this..." He trails off as he searches for the word, and then he finishes his thought as his palms graze up my thighs. His fingertips slide under the hiked up hem of my dress, and thrills dart through my chest that this is actually happening. "This *innocence* about you that I haven't encountered in a long time. Everybody always wants something from me, but you..." He shakes his head. "I think *I* want something from *you* this time."

I raise a brow that he can't see beneath the cat mask I'm still wearing. "What do you want?" I ask softly.

He leans forward and catches my lips with a soft kiss that sets my chest on fire. "Your innocence," he growls, and my God I nearly climax just from the heat of his words.

"You can have it," I say, and I don't know where the courage comes from, but I lift my hands to cup his face in my palms. His jaw is covered in this hot as fuck stubble that tickles my hands, but it's a stark reminder that this isn't just some dream. His eyes still hold that hot intensity on mine, and I don't know if I've ever wanted anything as much as I want Jack Dalton in this moment.

I lean forward and press my lips to his, and he simply takes over in the kind of way he probably does in every situation in his life. We kiss like our lives depend on it.

Someone opens the door, because the volume turns up on the music...but then it's quiet again. He flips us so one heartbeat later I'm pinned beneath him. The sudden move takes my breath away, but I don't have time to catch it because he's kissing me and I'm giving him everything I have back. He pauses for just a moment to get up and lock the door. When he returns, he resumes exactly where we left off.

His kiss is slow and sensual, and it's filled with an urgency that matches the way he thrusts his hips to mine. His hand moves along my thigh again, and this time he fingers the hem of my panties. Anticipation builds in my chest as need blooms down low.

He moves his lips from my mouth to my jaw, trailing down to my neck, and I shiver as he hits the little spot behind my ear that drives me wild.

I feel his smile against my neck as he discovers the things I like, and when his hand moves up to cup my breast, I push my chest more fully into it with a soft moan.

He trails back to my lips, and his tongue brushes mine, lighting a volcano of need inside me.

I can't believe this is really happening. It's like something out of a movie. Ordinary girl meets hot bachelor athlete everybody in the world wants, they screw on the couch in the club, and they live happily ever after.

Or something along those lines. Maybe it's something out of a dream. Certainly out of my wildest fantasies.

Except we're not screwing yet.

He reaches up and pulls my mask off, and he leans back a little to get a good look at me. His eyes move around my face before connecting back with mine. "Without the mask...even more gorgeous."

"You're smooth," I tease, and he chuckles.

"You haven't seen anything yet."

I laugh, but his mouth covers mine again and this time when he reaches down and fingers the hem of my panties, he pushes them aside. He runs a finger through me before he pushes it in, and holy *shit* those fingers know what they're doing.

He kisses me as he slides his finger in deeper, and then his mouth trails toward my neck. "God, I want you," he groans. "I want this." He thrusts his hips against my thigh, and I feel the steel package in his pants begging for escape.

His words and his body combine with his woodsy, manly scent and the absolute lust I feel for him, pushing me right over the edge way too quickly. My entire body seems to squeeze tightly against him all at once, and then pulse after pulse of pleasure washes over me.

"I want this, too." I fight to say the words through my climax because even in my totally incoherent state of bliss, I still know what I want. And I tell him. "I want *you.*"

He moves off me while I recover, and my eyes are closed while I try to catch my breath. I assume he's getting a condom, and his warmth covers me a beat later as he returns to nuzzle my neck. He sits up and pulls my panties down my legs.

"I've never been with a cat burglar before," he says.

"I've never been with a quarterback."

He raises a brow and offers a sly smile. "You won't be able to say that anymore after tonight."

He hovers over me and pulls his dick out of his jeans, and I gasp a little as I get a peek of the goods as he rolls on a condom just before he slams it into me.

Holy.

Shit.

My eyes roll back as I lie there and take him in. It's pleasure on top of perfection.

He thrusts into me again and again, and being with an athlete is so different from being with any of my exes. He's got strength and stamina as he holds himself up on one arm while he grabs my breasts over my costume. Then he reaches down between us to touch my clit while he continues to thrust.

He flips us in the middle of the action so he's sitting beneath me and I'm on his lap. His hands move under my ass as he directs our pace, and he buries himself as far inside me as he can before he pulls out and repeats the process. He reaches for the bottom of my dress and pulls it over my head, and then he unhooks my bra as I continue to move over him.

He pulls my body toward him so he can suck on my nipples while I move, his big hands wrapped around my back as he holds me to him. He's working every possible zone on my body as he grunts his way through our tryst, and all I can do is push my breasts more fully into his mouth and continue grinding my hips over his as I wrap my arms around him for balance.

His hands move to my shoulders, where he pushes me down a little harder, and he leans up to catch my lips with his. He pulls back, and I open my eyes to find his on mine. It's carnal and visceral, a contrast to the fact that he's screwing me on a couch. We're strangers doing something so illicit in a public place and anyone could walk in at any moment if that door isn't really locked, yet I don't know if I've ever felt as safe and protected as I do in this stranger's arms.

Something passes between us as our eyes hold the other's, some inexplicable connection that's full of tenderness and intimacy. It's hot and it's sexy and it's affectionate and warm all at the same time.

All the pleasure is too much.

I explode into another orgasm, and he catches my breast in his mouth before he follows right behind me. As he comes, he sucks even harder on my nipple, and *God* it feels so damn good that I can't help but scream out his name.

I'm so incoherent I'm pretty sure I actually say his *full* name, which is beyond embarrassing.

"Oh my God, Jack Dalton!"

And when it's all over, and my body stops contracting over his and he stops grunting and plowing into me, we both relax into each other for a few beats. He pushes me back just a little, and his eyes meet mine. I wrap my arms around his neck and he tightens his arms around my torso as a strangely hot and intimate moment passes between us. He's still inside me as we stare into each other's eyes quietly reveling in the feel of the other. He tips his chin up and brushes a soft kiss to my mouth.

We're strangers by definition, but we just did something so incredible and so intimate together that I know I will never forget.

Maybe he does this all the time, but I have to think it was unforgettable to him, too.

A knock at the door knocks reality back into me.

He growls out a quiet, "Fuck," before he shifts us to break our connection. "They only bother me when I need to get moving."

His words clue me into the fact that I'm not unique.

The thought of that sends a ripple of disappointment through me.

He closes doors at nightclubs and he's bothered when he's needed *all the time*. This is just another run of the mill Friday night for Jack Dalton, but it was a hell of a lot more than that for Kate Harmon.

I stand and locate my dress and my mask as my knee screams at me from the fall earlier. I get dressed and gather up my boots into my arms.

He draws in a deep breath then lets it out slowly before he stands. He finds a tissue to get rid of the condom and he fixes his pants and belt before he heads toward the door. He looks back at me to make sure I'm decent before he opens it.

The guy at the door says something close to Jack's ear, something I can't hear from this far away. I try to pretend I'm totally unaffected I'm just another notch in his belt as I clutch my boots in my hands, but I'm not that good of an actress.

The truth is I *am* affected. Deeply. I've never done this sort of thing before in my entire life, but between the Fireball and the lust, I jumped before I looked.

That's sort of my mantra, I suppose. Leap first, look later. It's why I'm twenty-five and going back to school while I work a job that isn't my end goal.

He glances back at me, and I get the distinct impression that the guy at the door is talking about me. Jack nods, and then he turns in my direction. He walks slowly toward me before he draws in a deep breath, and his entire demeanor has changed. He's no longer the hot quarterback who just hooked up with me. Now there's a tightness around his eyes that wasn't there before. It's only after he says his next words that I realize maybe it's guilt. "My, uh...*girlfriend* just showed up."

My heart skips a beat as my chest tightens. "You have a girlfriend?"

What. The. Fuck.

I feel like a total and complete fool. Of course he has a girlfriend. This is Jack Dalton. He probably has twenty of them.

"Sort of. I mean, she's pregnant, and I'm going through some things and making terrible decisions left and right and you shouldn't have been another one of them."

"I'm just a *bad decision* to you?" I repeat as his words sting me.

"No! No. That's not what I meant."

I blow out a breath. "I'll save you the trouble of trying to explain," I hiss.

I'll go find Shannon. I'll pretend none of this ever happened. I'll act like I'm not completely humiliated by this asshole who plays with women and their emotions regardless of what I thought I was getting into.

As I hobble out of the room armed with knee-high black boots gathered up in one arm and half a glass of Fireball in the other hand, I stop by the door where he still stands. "Go Aces. I hope you lose on Sunday."

I don't wait for his response. Instead, I stalk away from this private suite so I can find a quiet spot to put my shoes back on before the heat behind my eyes tips onto my cheeks.

CHAPTER 3

Four Months Later

I glance in my mirror, and the black truck is right on my tail.

Again.

Look, dude, we're all just trying to get wherever it is we're going, and I can't change the fate of the stoplights.

It turns green, and I hesitate just an extra second. Maybe it's me being a little on the passive aggressive side since clearly Black Truck is in a hurry, but he can relax.

He doesn't relax, though.

Before I take my foot off the brake pedal, he honks his horn.

Okay, buddy. You want to play? Let's play.

I ignore the sage advice from my father warning me of idiots on the road. I forget about that whole road rage thing he talked about when I was sixteen, and instead I hold up my middle finger so Black Truck can see it clearly though the back window of my little Kia.

My heart pounds wildly in my chest as adrenaline rushes through me.

This isn't really me—flipping the bird to strangers on the road like this, but it's my last day at my job and maybe I'm a little on the defensive side this morning.

I finally ease my foot off the brake and start moving. There's enough traffic this early in the morning that he can't exactly dart into the next lane to pass me, so he's stuck behind me.

I move a little slower than I normally would. There are cars up ahead anyway, so it's not like we're going far. I have plenty of time, and I can afford to drive extra cautiously in all this big traffic. Or, you know, to drive so as to piss off the asshole behind me.

I guess a space big enough for his enormous truck opens in the right lane, because he threads that needle and darts over.

Seriously. Who needs a truck that big on these busy little suburban roads?

He revs his engine to dart past me, and I look over at him just as he passes by. His windows are tinted, but I can still see him flip the bird back to me as he stares me down...or at least I assume he's staring me down, but I can't really tell since he's wearing a hat and sunglasses.

I flip my middle finger for the second time as my heart pounds.

Asshole.

Whatever. I'm almost to my destination anyway. I can see my left turn lane a few hundred feet away.

He glides in front of me, nearly clipping the front of my car as he cuts me off, and then he eases into the turn lane.

My turn lane.

My stomach does a little flip as I wonder just for a beat if he's going to the same Dunkin' Donuts I'm going to.

And now he's going to think I'm following him because he's going the same way I am. I study all the features of what must be some special edition Dodge truck. It has black trim and black accents everywhere, including the Ram logo across the back tailgate and blacked out windows all around.

I follow at a safe distance behind him through the parking lot of the mini-mall all the way toward the Dunkin' located on the far end, my eyes focused the entire way on the license plate. JD5.

He finally comes to a stop in the space immediately in front of the store, and I'm relegated to the back row.

Now I'm just pissed. I should draw in a calming breath and let it roll off me, but I'm not in the mood for this shit this morning.

Instead, I grab my purse from the passenger seat and toss my door open.

The door to the store is just closing behind the man driving JD5, and I stalk across the parking lot as my blood boils.

A loud ding greets me as I enter the store, and I spot the back of his head as he orders. Fury rages inside me as I pin my eyes on his tall, lean frame. We're the only two customers in here, and I catch all of "two large black coffees" before the rage inside me boils over.

"What kind of dick drives like that to get one person ahead at a Dunkin' Donuts?" I yell at the man in front of me. My hands are shaking and my knees are about to give out and what am I doing? What if this guy is dangerous? It's not like the teenager behind the counter is going to jump between us to save me. "What the hell is wrong with you?" I continue despite the thoughts in my mind telling me not to.

He turns slowly around, and I catch the smirk on full lips and the sculpted cheekbones and the perfectly straight nose before my eyes move up to meet his. His are a dark, stormy blue and quite familiar.

I freeze.

They're eyes I used to fantasize about, but they turned into eyes I couldn't stand looking at. They're eyes that bring the immediate sting of Halloween night last year right back to me as if I'm back in the moment when he told me he had a girlfriend. They're eyes that cause conflicting emotions to plow through me as I relive the most mortifying moment of my life paired with one of the steamiest, sexiest, hottest ones.

My blood boils over even more. I thought he was just some random asshole tailgating me, but this new twist is even worse. He's not just some random asshole.

He's a random celebrity asshole who once threw me out of a private suite at a nightclub after he screwed me. All those awful feelings of being dismissed from his suite rise to the surface and feel just as fresh as the night it happened.

His eyes light with a bit of recognition as he tilts his head, but he sort of looks like he can't quite place me. "Some people have places to be and don't have all day to fuck around behind the wheel driving their Kia like my grandmother would," he says.

"Mr. Dalton, will there be anything else?" the cashier behind the counter asks.

He turns back to the counter and orders some donuts. "Add whatever this young lady orders to my tab." He turns toward me and winks with his smirk firmly back in place.

Young lady? Excuse me, but I'm a twenty-five-year-old woman.

I let out a very unladylike snort. "Uh, that won't be necessary," I say to the cashier. "I don't need some asshole paying for me."

"Nonsense," he says, unfazed by my insult. "It's the least I can do."

I roll my eyes, and the poor high school kid behind the counter looks monumentally confused but ultimately gives this win to the jerk rather than to me.

Of course he does.

Because if there's anything I know about Jack Dalton, it's that he's a champion. He always wins.

He helps carry everything I ordered to the car (which, for the record, was only supposed to be one coffee and a dozen donuts), and I slide into the driver's seat and start the car. I roll down my window as he turns to leave, and I snarl at him a little. "Go Aces," I hiss, and he tilts his head again as if he recalls some distant memory.

Those were the same words I said to him when we parted the first time, most likely in the same snarl.

He laughs and shakes his head as I peel out of the parking lot.

And that's how I ended up with four dozen donuts and enough carafes of coffees to satisfy the entire staff at Kennedy's school on a Thursday morning.

CHAPTER 4

"Miss Kate!" Kennedy screeches when I walk into her kindergarten classroom armed with the boxes of donuts.

I grin as she runs over to me. "I saved you one of the special strawberry ones with sprinkles just in case you weren't first in line." I tap her nose, and she wraps her little arms around my legs.

"Whoa, Kate, that's a lot of donuts," Shannon says as she saunters up behind me and surveys everything I brought.

I shrug. "I figured they wouldn't go to waste in the faculty lounge. I have three carafes of coffee in the car, too, plus the one I brought for you."

"You didn't have to go to all that trouble." She takes out some paper plates and napkins while her aide starts to get the kids lined up.

"It's Kennedy's last day. She deserves some special treatment. And boy do I have a story for you." I'll fill her in later. She's literally the only human being alive who knows I had a one-night stand with Jack Dalton, and she happens to be my best friend.

She narrows her eyes at me, and I just smile and pretend to zip my lips. She laughs as she shakes her head.

The kids get their donuts, and I hang around while they eat them so I can help clean up. And then I head out so they can finish their school day. I pick up the almost two-year-old from his morning daycare and get him home for his nap, and just as he starts to wake, it's time to go pick up Kennedy.

I've managed to get the perfect routine down, and it only took me two years of being a live-in nanny for this family to do it.

And now they're moving from Vegas all the way across the country to Hartford, Connecticut, which means I'm kind of out of a job. But Shannon has offered me a place to stay on the couch she shares with her fiancé, Kevin, while I regroup and find a new job, so while I'm sad about one door closing, I'm excited about the potential new doors. I'm nothing if not a glass-half-full kind of girl.

The Van Astors treat me to a decadent salmon dinner courtesy of their cook along with a glass of Mrs. Van Astor's favorite wine for each of us, and then I help get the kids down to sleep for my final night with them. Mr. and Mrs. Van Astor have work to do, but they both wish me well as I go to bed for the last time in the room I've lived in as I've taken care of their children.

We say our tearful goodbyes in the morning, and they promise to keep in touch, and I promise to write, and that's it.

I hop into my little Kia with two large duffel bags and three large suitcases, pretty much the sum of my belongings since I sold all my furniture before I started this job, and I head toward Shannon's apartment.

I call my mom on the way.

"All done?" she answers.

"Yeah," I say, my tone subdued.

"You could come back home to Kansas," she says.

I bite back a laugh. No way in *hell* I'm going back to the small town my parents still call home. "And leave the palm trees and sunshine behind? Not on your life."

It's only a small part of why I didn't want to go to Hartford. Snow and clouds and rain and slush and scraping windshields...no thanks. I'll keep my independence and stick to the desert paradise of Las Vegas, thank you very much.

"Will you go back to psychology?" she asks.

I know she's hopeful since she and my dad paid for my degree, but working as a psychologist just wasn't a good fit for me. When I read about how live-in nannies had the opportunity to make *bank*, I gave up my job for a nanny position, and it only took a few weeks of living with the Van Astors to realize where my true passions lie.

And no, it's not in being a nanny, though I actually *loved* working with Kennedy and Miles.

My passion is in interior design.

It's in colors and light and textures and piecing them all together into some cohesive, aesthetically pleasing whole.

And so I'm slowly working toward a second degree. With just two online classes on my load per semester since that was all I had time for while nannying full-time, I feel like I might never finish. According to my advisor, though, I should be done in another eighteen months at this pace.

I basically got an apprenticeship by watching Mrs. Van Astor run her business. I learned about the reality of interior design, which is actually firmly based in architecture rather than in home décor, though I have to admit that home décor is a close second to my passion for design. Who doesn't love binging *House Hunters* and all those house flipping shows?

I'd like to go to school full time and finish my degree faster, but my ultimate dream is to open my own design firm, and I need a bankroll to do that. Nannying provides that bankroll. My salary from the Van Astors went entirely to my savings account since my room, board, and bills were taken care of. My only expenses were the necessities, my own entertainment, school, and my phone.

I'm working hard to set up the sort of future I want for myself, and I won't let anything get in my way.

"I'm not planning on it," I say to my mom, and I keep talking as not to give her a chance to try to convince me to use my degree. "I'm on my way to Shannon's now, and as soon as I get my laptop fired up, I'm going to search for new nanny positions."

"New nanny positions? Not back to being a school psychologist?" she presses.

I thought I'd be helping kids in my role as a school psychologist. Instead, I was chasing paperwork and helping the counselors with their overflow work, which meant during the end of the school year I was scheduling kids for the next year, double checking class sizes, and calling parents to let them know why their kid didn't get into the honors program.

To be fair, I *did* help a lot of kids. It just turned out working in a school wasn't for me.

I sigh. "I'm using my degree every single day with the kids in my charge, Mom. It's just not in the traditional sort of way. And I make *way* more money doing this."

"As long as you're happy," she says.

"I am. You know how much I love Vegas."

And I am.

For the most part.

I have a good friend in Shannon. I have money in the bank. I'm working toward my goals.

But...

As my mom would say, it's not all peaches and carrot cake.

I'm hopelessly single. My last boyfriend turned out to be a real dick. I haven't been with a man since Halloween, and we all know how that turned out.

I'm out of a job.

I really just need something for the next eighteen months or so where I can live in somebody else's house to do my job so I don't have to pay rent. Would working in interior design be a better fit than being a nanny? Probably. But the paychecks would be smaller, and I'd have to find a place to live, which would mean far more expenses.

Being a live-in nanny isn't easy since you're living where you're working, but I established a routine and ran the Van Astor house like a machine. It helps that I'm good with kids, obviously, but dealing with parents is a different beast entirely. I was lucky with my former employers, and I'd still be with them if they weren't relocating.

My parents told me I could choose any college I wanted when I was a senior in high school, and something about Las Vegas always called to me. So I moved to start college at the University of Nevada Las Vegas at the ripe age of eighteen, and seven years later I'm not planning on leaving...not even for the Van Astors.

I'll find something. Mrs. Van Astor told me she'd leave me a glowing recommendation with the agency they found me through, and I have faith I'll get another job.

Fingers crossed it's sooner rather than later.

"I do, honey. And maybe I don't say it enough, but I'm proud of you for following your dreams. I wish I had the guts to do that when I was your age."

I'm surprised and a little touched by her words. "It's never too late," I say. I can't help but wonder what her dreams are. She and my dad run the diner that's been in my dad's family for generations, and I always just assumed that was her dream.

Her only reply is a soft sigh, and then I'm pulling into Shannon's complex.

"I better run, but we'll talk soon, okay?" I say.

"Love you, Katie bug."

"Love you, too, Mama bug."

She chuckles and I cut the call, and then I use the key Shannon gave me yesterday to let myself into her place.

I lug my suitcases and duffel bags into her family room, where I'll be living for the (hopefully short) foreseeable future, and then I plop on the couch and open my laptop to start my new job search.

CHAPTER 5

"Where's Kevin?" I ask as I heap my taco with shredded cheese. Shannon decided to treat me to tacos, my number one favorite food in the universe, and we've paired our dinner with margaritas, chips, and salsa.

"He went to a happy hour with some friends so we could have a girl's night," Shannon says.

"How's the wedding planning coming along? What can I do?"

"I think we're all set." She shrugs. "We're less than two months away now and now we sort of just rely on everyone we've paid to do the things we're paying them to do."

"Thanks for letting me stay here in the midst of all this. I'm going to pound the pavement and find something soon to get out of your hair."

"You know Kev and I both adore you," she says affectionately. "Stay forever if you want."

I wrinkle my nose. "I definitely don't want to hang around for the wedding night."

She waggles her eyebrows. "Babe, every night's like a wedding night around here lately."

"Save the details. But I'm happy for you." And not at all jealous.

I glance at the rock on the third finger of her left hand.

Okay...maybe a *little* jealous.

I'm hopelessly single at the moment. Blake couldn't handle seeing me only once a week on my night off, so he got his rocks off elsewhere. I don't know why he didn't just end it with me before cheating on me, but he did what he did and I'm better off without him. We broke up about a week before the quarterback who shall not be named screwed me on his couch while *he* had a girlfriend, too.

Men suck.

It's hard meeting someone new when you're working all the time, even harder meeting someone decent and worth my time. And that's why I've decided to put my love life on the backburner so I can save money to fulfill my dreams.

They say you meet *The One* when you're least expecting it, and I have zero expectations (or prospects) at the moment.

All those thoughts lead me back to what happened yesterday, and I gasp as I realize I haven't told Shannon yet. "Oh my God. You will *never* guess who I ran into yesterday morning."

Shannon narrows her eyes at me from across her kitchen table. "Adam Levine?"

I laugh. "No. But close."

She raises her brows in surprise. "Close?"

"Jack. Motherfucking. Dalton." I punctuate each word as I say it.

She drops half a taco on her plate, spilling the contents everywhere. "No way! Tell me everything!"

I launch into the story of the guy who was tailing me on the drive for donuts. "I stormed into the store and started yelling at the guy and when he turned around, it was unmistakably him."

"Holy shit," she murmurs. "Did he remember you?"

"No." I shake my head. "At least I don't think he did. I said *go Aces* when I left and he sort of looked at me like some memory came up, and then I remembered I said the same thing to him after he kicked me out."

"You're just bitter because of the meme."

I purse my lips at the mention of what followed my night with Jack Dalton. "The meme that you shall remain silent upon for the remainder of your life."

She nods and flips a hand at me. "Yeah, yeah, yeah, until death do us part or else death *will* do us part," she says, repeating my threats back at me.

"I'm glad my threats have stuck after all this time," I deadpan.

"Well you did say you'd kill me if I ever told anybody, so a girl tends to take those kinds of things seriously," she quips. "Tell me you at least exchanged numbers with him."

I snort. "Hardly. Instead I loaded up on extra donuts since he offered to pay for my order. I felt like it was the least he could do."

A lightbulb seems to go off over her head. "Ahh. *That* was why you had so many donuts." She giggles. "So that was it?"

I nod. "That was it."

"You didn't mention the meme?"

I shoot her a look. "Uh, that would be a negative, my friend. I have never mentioned the meme to anybody ever, and I never will." I glare at her. "And you better not, either."

She rolls her eyes at my warning. "I feel like the fallout from all that was *way* worse for him than it was for you."

"I know it was," I agree. "But that's only because I was wearing a mask with my cat burglar costume and he was, well, Jack Dalton. Everybody knew who he was *and* he had a girlfriend."

I think back to that stupid night.

I guess when the door opened while we were making out on the couch, someone snapped pictures of us. The one that's been cemented into pop culture history turned out to be an incredibly unattractive photo of me looking like I'm trying to steal his tongue out of his mouth with mine.

The image haunts me to this day, and if he wasn't Jack Dalton, nobody would've given it a second glance. But because he's a celebrity, it turned into a viral sensation overnight when someone cleverly captioned the photo.

Shannon nods, and then she bursts into giggles out of the clear blue. "The cat burglar's stealing Jack Dalton's tongue!"

I purse my lips and stare at her. "It's not funny."

"It's freaking hilarious," she says, and now she's laughing so hard tears are starting to fall from her eyes. "You were dressed as a *cat burglar*."

I sigh and set my taco down, my appetite suddenly gone as I remember the complete mortification of what happened followed by the stupid meme going viral the next day. That meme was *everywhere* in the days that followed, and every time I saw it, I felt the sting of rejection. I couldn't escape it no matter how hard I tried.

I made Shannon swear never to tell a soul it was me, and then I promptly chopped my long, wavy hair nearly to my chin and highlighted it so it wasn't quite as dark as it was before. Voila. New person nobody would ever recognize by her hair in a meme.

Thank God for stupid costumes with masks.

I'm just thankful Jack didn't seem to recognize me. I guess the haircut helped, probably added to the fact that I started dying it different shades. I tried platinum, but it wasn't for me, and now I've settled on an earthy and warm amber shade that seems to make my hazel eyes really pop.

Eventually she stops laughing. We finish our dinner, we drink margaritas, we gossip about all the teachers at the school where I used to work—the same one where Shannon still works—and then we call it a night.

Even though Kevin is quiet when he comes in a little after one in the morning, he still wakes me up. I pretend he doesn't, but it's just another reminder that I need a new job.

Stat.

I can't sleep on Shannon's couch forever, nor do I want to.

But in the days that follow, I can't find a thing.

Nobody is looking for a live-in nanny in this general area.

There are tons of nanny positions available, but they're all missing that key component of having my rent paid for while I work.

This is my big, grand plan. Focus on my career. Finish my degree. Save money to work toward my goals. It was all working so well, and then the Van Astors had to go and move away on me.

I throw myself into my schoolwork. I'm acing all my classes. I help Shannon with wedding planning.

A week passes, and my back is stiff from sleeping on the couch.

I take a part-time gig at Old Navy mostly for the discount but also so I can contribute to Shannon's rent and not totally drain the savings I've built over the last two years. I volunteer for the closing shifts to give the betrothed couple some private evening time away from me, and it has significantly cut down on my need to use my noise-canceling headphones.

And another week goes by. I've taken to hanging out at Starbucks and Panera just to give Shannon and Kevin more space, but it's ten at night and I'm sulking on the couch also known as my bed with my laptop on my lap, scrolling all the local sites I know that might possibly have a listing for a live-in nanny.

Still nothing.

"What are you going to do?" Shannon asks.

I narrow my eyes at her. "Are you trying to get rid of me?"

"Of course not, babe. But this couch ain't that comfy."

I laugh. "I guess I need to set an end date for this and if nothing happens, I start applying for open elementary school psychologist positions for the fall."

It's not what I want, and I can't seem to force myself to even look at school websites to see if I can find an open position. It feels too much like giving up my dreams, and besides, it's spring. Even my shitty back-up plan of applying to school districts won't have a position that starts for several months.

"Oh, Kate. I know how much you hated it. We'll find you something," she says, and then her eyes light up like a lightbulb just went off. "And in the meantime, let's get you laid."

I laugh and hold up a hand. "I'm good, really. I can't exactly screw a guy on your couch."

"So you'll go back to his place." She shrugs. "Come on. At least join one of those dating apps. I need to live vicariously through you."

I narrow my eyes at her. "You're getting *married* to the man of your dreams in six weeks, Shan. You have a job you adore. I think if anyone gets to live vicariously around here, it's not you."

"My friend Alison met her husband on Tinder," she hints.

"That's wonderful for Alison. I'm Kate, and I don't need a man to make me happy."

Though the couch is awful lonely and the last guy I had sex with was Jack Dalton. It's not like I'm saving myself to have sex with him again.

But it was one hell of a damn good time before he mentioned the whole girlfriend thing.

"I'm just trying to pull you out of this funk, girl," she says.

"I'm not in a funk!" I protest.

"Spoken like a girl truly in the middle of a funk." She purses her lips as she studies me. "Fine. No Tinder. But Kev has a friend at work who's super cute. Would you consider maybe meeting him for a drink that could end up back at his place?"

"God, you're really desperate to get rid of me," I say.

She lifts a shoulder. "Maybe just for, like, *one* night..."

"I've overstayed my welcome." My tone is flat, and I'm not mad at her. I'm mad at myself for sleeping on a couch for two weeks sitting in my own feelings rather than trying harder to get out of her hair. "I'll take on more shifts at Old Navy and see if I can find a place to rent, okay?"

"I don't want you to do that," she says. "I'm mostly teasing you. I love having you around. It's like a sleepover every night."

I give her a wry smile. Who in their right mind would want a sleepover *every night*? "Thanks for letting me stay here. I'll find something soon. Promise."

"And Kev's friend?" she presses.

I roll my eyes and blow out a breath. "Set it up."

CHAPTER 6

Shannon gave me Kevin's friend's number, and he texted me first asking if I'd like to meet for a drink. I agreed to afternoon coffee rather than an evening drink, and I chose Starbucks because hell if I want to chance running into number five on the Broncos at some other coffee location.

That's the extent of our texting conversation thus far, and I'm a little nervous. I have no idea what Vince looks like, but according to Shannon, he'll be wearing a black shirt and he's super cute. When I walk in, I take a quick survey of the place. My eyes land on a cute guy in a black shirt who's looking at me with a bit of reticence.

That's definitely the guy, and Shannon was right. He's cute. *Super* cute. Dark eyes hidden behind black frames that make him look both sexy and intellectual, short, dark hair, a strong jawline, nice forearms. That's about all I can see of him since he's sitting, but so far, so good.

I cross my fingers this is my guy.

I walk up to the table. "Vince?"

His lips widen into a smile as he nods. "Kate?"

"That's me." I pull the chair out and sit, the idea of actually ordering coffee long forgotten as nerves about this date start to take over.

"Nice to meet you," he says, and I smile.

"And you." A beat of awkward quiet passes between us, and then I ask, "So you work with Kevin?"

He nods. "We're in the same accounting division."

"He's marrying my best friend," I blurt.

"You're a bridesmaid, right?" he asks.

I nod. "Will you be there?"

"I'm a groomsman."

"With a plus one?" God, how desperate am I?

He laughs and shakes his head. "No. Just me. One of the other guys in our department is going solo, too, so at least I'll have someone to talk to."

I give him a wink. "Maybe two people."

He grins, and I excuse myself to order a drink. I decide to fire off a quick text to Shannon even though I'm next to order, and I tease Shannon in my message even though I've only known this guy a total of sixty seconds.

Me: *Good work, Shan. He's a hottie. Thinking our coffee date may end at his place. Hope his bed is comfier than your couch because I think I really see a future in it. Wedding bells, kids, the whole works.*

I head up to the counter to order, and I glance over at the table after I pay. Vince is on his phone while he waits for me, and he glances up at me before his eyes move back down to his phone.

I wait at the counter, and I check my phone to see I don't have a reply from Shannon yet.

"Order for Kate!" the barista yells, and I grab my coffee and head back to my date, excited to get to know him even though I don't *really* think I'll be sharing a bed with him the day I met him.

I did that once. It didn't work out well.

"I'm so sorry," he says as I join him at the table again. He stands. "I need to go."

My brows dip. "Is everything okay?"

"Yeah," he says, and he seems flustered. "It's fine. I just, uh, have a thing..."

It's an excuse, and a poor one at that, but I'm not going to *force* him to sit with me. "Right, okay then. It was nice meeting you."

"You too." He barely squeaks out the words before he bolts, and I can't help but sit in epic confusion for a beat as I try to reconcile what the hell just happened.

Surprise follows the shock, and then sadness creeps in as tears heat behind my eyes.

It's *me*.

There's something fundamentally undatable about *me* or else this guy wouldn't have just bolted mere seconds after meeting me. My confidence takes a total dive right off the cliff. It's barely back since that night with Jack, and this pretty much crushes it.

I click open the camera on my phone and check my face. Nothing in my teeth. No eye crusties. No lipstick on my teeth. Hair all in place, a cute sundress from Old Navy...

Sadness transitions over to anger.

What the hell happened from the smiling introductions and the promise of a little bit of flirting that might last us all the way to Shannon and Kevin's wedding next month to him walking out just now?

I open my texts to let Shannon know she picked a real dick for me when I spot the problem.

My heart stops.

My chest tightens.

That text I sent while I was in line.

It didn't go to Shannon.

It went to Vince.

I set my hand over my face in total embarrassment as I blow out a breath.

It was a joke! Just a joke!

But sweet, kind, super cute Vince couldn't have known that, and I scared the shit out of him with that text about wedding bells and kids and sleeping at his place.

God, I am *such* an idiot sometimes.

Is this rock bottom? It feels like it.

And there goes another week.

And another.

Still, I have no job prospects. No dating prospects. Hell, I don't even *want* to try dating after that last disaster. Kevin explained what happened to Vince, that it was all just a joke, but I guess he swiped right on some girl and he has decided to plow forward with her rather than the terrifying woman that is me.

It's been a full month of mooching off my best friend and I have to get the hell out of here for all our sakes. Shannon keeps giving me sad little looks that are supposed to be sympathetic but instead just remind me how damn far down I have fallen.

I need to take control back.

And then, the ringing of my phone wakes me bright and early at seven in the morning.

I click it off when I don't recognize the number.

I close my eyes to go back to sleep, but a voicemail notification dings a minute later.

I decide to have a listen.

"This is Lily Park calling on behalf of Calvin Bennett of the Vegas Aces. I'm looking for Kathryn Harmon with a potential job opportunity. Please call me back at your earliest convenience." She leaves her phone number.

I stare at my phone for a beat, and then I replay the message.

It says the same thing the second time.

I scramble to call her back.

The *Vegas Aces* have a job opportunity? Like the football team?

For *me*?

"Lily Park," the same voice who left the voicemail answers.

"Lily, hi, it's Kathryn Harmon returning your call."

"Thanks so much for getting back to me. Your information was given to Calvin Bennett, the owner of the Vegas Aces, by Charles Van Astor. Given your history in both psychology and dealing with children, Mr. Bennett has an, um, *unique* job proposition for you if you're still in the market."

Mr. Van Astor did this?

I mean, I guess it makes sense. He's well connected in the Las Vegas community, and he held season tickets. I guess I just didn't realize he and Cal were old pals. Whatever the case, I'm grateful for this opportunity. I'm desperate for anything at this point.

"Can you come down to the practice facility to hear more about it today at noon?" Lily asks.

"I'll be there," I say.

CHAPTER 7

It's a Saturday in the off-season, but I guess that doesn't mean the team owner ever stops working. You don't earn enough money to buy a football team without putting in the hours. It takes me all of five seconds to learn that Mr. Bennett started his career as a tax attorney, transitioned to real estate, and then sold his incredibly successful company only to buy the Aces a few years ago.

Shannon and Kevin prep me during and after breakfast. Kevin tells me everything I could possibly ever want to know about every player he knows on the Aces, not that I'll remember most of it. I'm a casual fan, and I know enough about the sport to make light conversation, so I feel okay with that end of it. I shower and head to the address Lily emailed me.

My curiosity burns as I pull into the parking lot. What sort of job could this man possibly have for me that involves psychology and looking after children?

Maybe one of his players needs a nanny.

Or maybe he needs someone to watch players' kids during practice.

But Lily said it was a unique position. Neither of those things would be *unique*.

Once I get to the parking lot and shut off my GPS, I take a deep breath. I read Lily's email once more then text her to let her know I'm here as per her directions.

Lily: *I'll meet you in the lobby.*

Sure enough, a woman a few years older than me waits for me in the lobby. Her chin-length black hair is cut in a perfect bob that swings as she approaches me.

"Kathryn?" she asks.

"Call me Kate, please. I assume you're Lily?"

She nods and reaches out her hand to shake mine. "Follow me."

We wind through a series of hallways and I see why she had me meet her in the lobby rather than give me directions to the owner's office. Once we arrive, though, I find Calvin Bennett sitting behind a formidable wooden desk, and he stands with a smile to greet me. He wears a black Aces polo shirt with khaki pants, and he looks more like a friendly uncle than the cutthroat businessman I've learned he is.

"Kathryn, thank you for coming today," he says, and I shake his hand across the desk.

"Thank you for inviting me, Mr. Bennett."

"Have a seat," he says, nodding toward a chair opposite him.

I do, and I perch awkwardly in it while I wait for him to explain what this is all about.

"Charles has been both my lawyer and my confidante for many years," he begins, and how did I not know that this man was one of Charles's clients? Maybe that whole client-attorney privilege thing. "When I spoke to him yesterday about a small issue I'm having, he couldn't recommend you highly enough."

"Me?" I ask, my hand flying to my chest in surprise.

He nods. "Tell me you're still in the market for a new job."

I chuckle. "Well, yes." I decide to go for honesty. "I don't have a new position yet. My plan was to find another nannying position, preferably live-in, to work for the next eighteen months or so while I finish my degree in interior design. Eventually, I'd like to open up my own firm."

"And the live-in position allows you to save money to do that?"

I nod.

"Smart girl," he says. He leans back in his chair casually and steeples his fingers in front of his mouth as he thinks for a few beats. Then he blows out a breath and leans forward. "Kathryn, let me be frank. I don't know you from anybody else, but Charles told me how he admired your determination and your strong will in dealing with his children. With your background in both psychology and caring for children, he gave me an idea. It's unconventional, but I'll compensate you well for it and if you can stick it out until February, I'll front you the money to open your design firm. Whatever you need."

My brows dip. "February?" I repeat stupidly. "That's ten months."

He nods. "Less than one year for a hundred grand plus whatever your startup costs are, no strings attached. In fact, rather than estimate what startups might cost you, I'll just call your salary two hundred thousand. We'll prorate it every two weeks for the next ten months, and you use it how you see fit, whether it's to create your new company or go back to school full time."

My jaw drops. "Two...two hund...hundred...two hundred th-thousand?" I stutter the words.

I have a decent amount of money saved after working for the Van Astors, and I was pretty damn proud of that number until I heard this one.

He's handing my company to me and all I have to do is agree to whatever he's about to ask me.

Um...duh. I don't even care what it is. Where do I sign? "What's the job?" I ask, forcing my logic into the front seat for a second.

"I have a player joining my team who needs some...how should I put this?" He wrestles with his words for a few beats, and it makes me nervous as to what, exactly, he's about to ask me. He clears this throat. "He's made some headlines. He's a star player, but he's been making some poor choices. He's not dangerous or anything. He's a good man. A *great* man. But he's been going through some things, and I want to help him straighten out again. Turn his life around, his *image* around, you know? Since he's new to this organization, I need him to know how we do things around here. I need someone to keep a close eye on him. And I'll kick in a fifty-K bonus if you keep him out of handcuffs for the next ten months."

My brows dip. "You want to pay me a quarter of a million dollars to babysit one of your players?"

"I was thinking the official title would be something more along the lines of *behavior coach*, but...yes. That's essentially what I'm looking for. I'd need you by his side pretty much twenty-four-seven. You'd be a live-in nanny to a thirty-something-year-old man. With your psychology background, you have the tools to help him. I'd be relying on you to help put his ego in the backseat so he can contribute to a winning team without all these other distractions getting in the way."

So he wants to pay the girl who is actually part of a viral cat meme to be the model of good behavior as a coach? Makes a whole lot of sense.

Thank God I had that mask on in that stupid meme.

I feel like I'm the punchline to some joke here, but Cal is dead serious across the desk. "I've only ever used my knowledge in the field when it comes to children," I admit, and wait just one hot minute...why the hell am I debating this point when he's offering me the kind of money he is?

Because of honesty, Kate.

Give it to him straight.

"Surely there's someone more qualified than I am," I say.

He presses his lips together. "That may well be, but I need someone immediately, and I need someone I trust. If Charles recommended you as someone who has cared for the two people most precious to him, that's all I need to know."

"Will there be anyone else around?" I ask. "Or would it just be me and this stranger?"

"He's engaged, and they have a baby. They're getting married this summer, so you'll have some time off around their honeymoon. A small staff will come and go from the house, and they have a nanny. So, yes, there will always be people around, and you'll have access to me as well as the entire coaching staff should any issues arise."

I stare at him and twist my lips as I try to decide what to do, but I already know the answer. I need a job. I want to save money. Those are my only two current goals, and this man is giving me both.

"Let me level with you, Kathryn," he says. "You'll be perfectly safe. While he did recently punch a teammate, he's not generally a violent guy, and certainly never against women."

"He...*punched* someone?"

"The guy had it coming, if I'm being honest." He folds his hands in front of him and looks at me in earnest. "I think it's part of why he wanted a trade deal. Look, he's lost a few things over the last few months that have taken a toll on him. He's emotionally fragile but won't admit it, and he's filling those voids with vices. I need you. I need someone to keep an eye on him and remind him everything he has to lose while coaching him to take accountability to see that what he's doing affects more than just himself. You'll be the angel on his shoulder fighting against the devils who seem to keep making his decisions for him."

I suck my top lip into my mouth and capture it between my teeth as I take all of three seconds to decide. What's the worst that can happen? So I keep a hot football player out of trouble for less than a year.

Okay, okay, he didn't say *hot*, but still. I can *totally* do that. "That's it? You don't need to interview me or anything?"

He chuckles. "What do you think this is?"

"An interview?" I guess.

"I haven't gotten to where I am without having a strong intuition about people. And you seem like the trustworthy type." He presses a few keys on his keyboard and clicks the mouse, and a document starts printing a few seconds later. He grabs it from his printer and passes it over. "Read it over, sign it, and leave it with Lily," he says.

"And just like that, I have a job that'll pay two hundred thousand dollars over ten months?"

He nods. "Plus that bonus if you keep my boy out of trouble. But you'll be working constantly, following him pretty much everywhere, and this won't be an easy task. He'll push back against you, surely. You'll start Monday pending your signature on that contract, and once you're in, you're in. There's no backing out. I have a meeting scheduled with the man you'll be coaching Monday morning at eight. He'll be staying at one of my houses for now, so come at nine to meet him and pick up your house key."

"Yes sir," I say.

I'm desperate.

I need a job where I don't have to pay rent, where I'm not sleeping on Shannon's couch, and where I can still take classes and save money.

I have no other options. It's already been a month, my savings is dwindling, my dreams are moving further and further away, and if I don't snatch up this position, someone else will.

I read over the contract that has a few more details about this new position, and I sign my life away for the next ten months with a flourish without *really* thinking things over.

Just like that, I have a job—one that'll pay me enough over the next ten months to launch my dreams as soon as I finish my degree.

And then some.

CHAPTER 8

"So what's the job?" Kevin asks before the door even closes behind me.

"This is all on the downlow since I actually signed a nondisclosure agreement, so you two aren't allowed to tell a soul." They both mock zip their lips, and then I lift a casual shoulder. "Apparently Calvin has some new guy on the team he wants me to babysit—er, uh, he wants me to be his *behavior coach*."

"Behavior coach?" Shannon asks. "Is that a real thing?"

I laugh. "Yes, it's a real thing, though it's unconventional to have a full-time behavioral coach. It's usually more of a once-a-week type appointment, but I'm not just coaching his behavior. I'm helping him make smart decisions. Basically I help him turn his behavior, and thus his image, around, and I keep him out of headlines and handcuffs."

"This is so freaking awesome," Kevin says. "Who is it?"

"I have no idea," I admit. "It sounds like whoever it is hasn't been publicly announced as the newest member of the Aces."

Shannon's brows dip doubtfully. "Is this a good idea?"

"Calvin said he's a good guy who's just been making bad decisions. It's not like he's dangerous or anything. I think it's fine."

"Will there be anyone else around?" Shannon asks.

I nod, proud of myself for actually knowing the answer to that question. "House staff, a fiancée, and a kid."

"Sounds like it'll be crowded," Kevin says.

"What about the wedding?" Shannon asks, and I force my eyes to stay steady on her and not roll them over the fact that she's bringing up the wedding *again*. I mean, I'm totally happy for her. I swear. But it's *all* we talk about lately. "Did you write into the contract that you need time off?"

Oh.

Shit.

I wasn't thinking straight when I signed that contract. I was like a cartoon character with dollar symbols for eyeballs. I was blinded by the lure of the cash and the desperation to have a job.

"You didn't," she says. She points a scary finger in my direction. "Kathryn Elizabeth Harmon, it's far too late to change the programs to delete you as a bridesmaid."

I hold up both hands. "It's fine, it's fine. I'll figure something out." Is there a babysitting service for adults? Can I find someone to fill my spot so I can attend events that were scheduled well before I took this job? Can I bring him with me to the wedding? Will he even go?

"Oh, wait!" she says, her eyes lighting up. "Bring him with! Can you imagine? A *real celebrity* at my wedding?"

"If it's what the bride wants, it's what the bride gets." As long as I can convince the football player in my charge to agree to it.

I push the feeling of utter mortification that I don't have a date to this shindig down, down, down.

This wedding is happening three weeks from yesterday, and I didn't even think to mention at my interview that I'll need time for the bachelorette party in two weeks plus all the wedding events in three weeks...and all the stuff Shannon will need help with leading up to the big day.

I'm sure I can find *some* time off. I'm sure he doesn't need *constant* supervision. How bad could he be?

Should I call Calvin?

No, I can't do that.

Maybe I can mention it on Monday morning.

Or maybe I can get someone else to watch him while I take part in these events.

I'm being paid to tag along with *him* wherever *he* is going, not the other way around. I'm not being paid to have a personal life, and the contract made that perfectly clear. I was okay with those terms when I signed it, but now I'm wondering whether I should've taken it with me and had someone else review it before I signed.

Too late.

It's only ten months.

It'll fly by.

I run with Shannon to her final wedding gown fitting, and we pick up her shoes and her veil. I play the part of a bridesmaid thrilled to be doing all the things with the bride even though I just want to go home, drink a margarita, and enjoy my last couple days of freedom with Netflix and pajama pants.

But even then I remember that *home* is currently Shannon's couch, so even at *home*, I can't escape all things Shannon's wedding.

Which is fine.

This is an exciting, (hopefully) once-in-a-lifetime event, and I will be there for my best friend every spare moment I possibly can be.

Which apparently means the entire rest of the weekend.

So even though I'm a bundle of nerves over the new position I'm starting on Monday, I don't get much chance to talk it out or even really think about it since we're flying from one vendor to the next, from one important decision to the next, from one hair trial appointment to the next.

And I will figure out a way to be at all the events so I can fully participate in everything I signed on for when I agreed to be her bridesmaid.

It isn't until Sunday night as I'm packing up my stuff that Shannon sits on the recliner beside the couch that I've been sleeping on the last month.

"Are you excited for your new job?" she asks.

"Thank you for asking," I begin. "And yeah, I'm excited. More nervous than excited."

"Nervous about what?"

I lift a shoulder as I stare down into my suitcase. "What if the guy's a real douche? Can I really do this for the ten months I've already committed to if I can't stand him?"

"Can you back out?" she asks.

I shrug. "Calvin said there's no backing out, but there's always a way. It'll just come with a pretty hefty fine."

"It's weird that you don't even know who it is."

"It doesn't really matter." I grab some eye shadow palettes to pack in my makeup bag. "Psychology is the study of the human mind and how it affects behaviors, and that's something I have experience with."

"Well, yeah, but with kids."

I nod, conceding. "I might be a little rusty, but I used psychology all the time when I worked with Kennedy and Miles. This man sounds like a grown-up throwing tantrums, and those are something I have quite a bit of experience dealing with."

"Dude, when I have kids, I'm coming to you for all the best parenting tips."

I giggle. "Let's just see how this all works out first."

CHAPTER 9

I'm focused on the road as I navigate my little Kia toward the practice facility on Monday morning. My suitcases are shoved into the trunk and the backseat is filled with my duffel bags. Today's not just the start of a new job. It's the start of a new residence for nearly the next year.

The radio is on, but I'm lost in my own thoughts until I hear a name that catches my attention. I turn the volume up a little to try to catch what they're talking about.

"...so many rumors swirling about him right now," the female deejay, DeeDee says.

Her counterpart, Rick, adds, "He was spotted at a strip club last night with Ben Olson."

"Ben Olson as in the newest tight end for the Aces?" DeeDee asks.

"The one and only," Rick says.

"You think Jack Dalton is in town visiting his brother? Or you think there's more to it?" DeeDee asks.

"Word on the street is that there may be more to it," Rick says. "I mean, his fiancée does live here. And speaking of the word on the street, after the break we'll play Street Smarts for tickets to see the Sin City Crue. This is Rick and DeeDee in the morning on Hot Ninety-Four-Three."

I turn the volume down as my chest starts to race.

I wonder if it's Ben Olson that I'm being hired to babysit—to *coach*. I saw his name on the list of players recently traded to the Aces.

You know who wasn't on that list? Jack Dalton.

I did my research this weekend. He hasn't been traded to the Aces. Once a trade goes through, it hits the media right away—at least that's what Kevin told me. And from what I know of Ben Olson, well, he's kind of a party guy. He might need someone to keep him on track.

He's freaking hot as hell, too, but that's beside the point.

It might even be fun to hang out with him if I wasn't going into this from a professional standpoint.

I park my car and I spot a big, black truck in the parking lot.

It's not just any big, black truck.

It's black all over, from the tinted windows to the black trim and black accents, and the license plate is familiar: *JD5*.

My chest tightens.

I know that truck.

I feel like this is one too many coincidences, and suddenly I have a really bad feeling about this new job I've been hired to do.

You know, the one I can't back out of.

Shit.

Shit, shit, shit.

I check in at the front desk then start my walk through the hallways I memorized the first time I came here. I wish this was a shorter walk, because right now my heart is racing and I feel like I don't have enough oxygen pumping inside of me to make it all the way there.

I'm so nervous, in fact, that I take a wrong turn and end up on totally the wrong end of the building.

I backtrack to try to figure out where I went wrong, and I feel tears heating behind my eyes at the sheer embarrassment of getting lost in this building. I'm going to be late to meet this person I'm coaching for the next ten months and is there really anything worse than showing up late on your first day when you've been hired to be the good example?

This is all wrong.

I'm a damn hot mess in my everyday life, let alone in a situation like this. Calvin hired the wrong psychologist for this job.

Just knowing Jack Dalton's truck out there is setting me on edge. It's *not* him. It *can't* be him.

Some older man with kind eyes nods a hello as he passes me down the hallway. "Can you help me find Calvin Bennett's office?" I ask, my voice riddled with sheer desperation.

"Of course," he says, and I follow him back the way I came. He walks me almost all the way there, and I can't help but express my eternal gratitude once I spot Lily's desk three minutes ahead of schedule.

My hands are shaking and my knees are knocking together as that bad feeling in my gut only worsens as Lily looks up at me. "Good morning, Ms. Harmon," she says brightly. "Mr. Bennett is waiting for you."

She nods for me to head right in.

I draw in a deep breath, rooted to the spot for a beat, and then I force one foot in front of the other as I move toward Calvin's office. As soon as I'm in the doorway, I spot the back of his head, and I immediately know.

Oh my God.

I close my eyes for a second as I try to wake up from this nightmare.

Jack Dalton isn't just some hot football star with a penchant for getting into trouble.

He's the guy who screwed me in a nightclub a few months ago and kicked me out when his girlfriend showed up.

And I've been hired to help him manage his decisions for nearly the next year.

I hate him.

I hate how freaking *hot* he looks sitting there casually in a white t-shirt and black shorts.

He's a huge presence even from behind. This may be Calvin's office, but he owns this room just like he owned that nightclub.

I hate that I can still remember what it felt like when his finger pushed into me and when he cupped my breast in his hand and when his tongue moved against mine. I hate that I still dream of him moving inside me and sometimes when I touch myself I pretend it's him.

I hate that he was such an asshole.

God, I don't think any man has ever raised such conflicting feelings in me.

My only hope here is that he doesn't recognize me. If he does, then it's game over.

"Kathryn, good morning," Calvin says, and at his words, Jack turns around.

My heart stops beating for a second as our eyes connect. I swear to God there's this heat that passes between us, but it's probably only me who feels it. His eyes are navy blue and stormy, and they widen as they fall onto me with a bit of recognition.

There goes that ray of hope, but then his single word restores it a little as his lips broaden into a smile. "Kia!"

He recognizes me from our run-in at Dunkin' the other day...*not* from our one night together. It was dark, and I had a mask on for most of it. But God help me if he ever figures out that I was the one he fucked on a couch last Halloween before we became a viral cat meme together.

"It's Kathryn," I grit out between my clenched jaw, and then I force it to loosen as I realize nobody on planet Earth ever calls me Kathryn. "Kate, actually."

"You two know each other?" Calvin asks.

"We had a, um, run-in at Dunkin' Donuts the other day," I explain.

I sure as hell don't mention Halloween, but Jack's eyes flick to my chest before his eyes rise to mine. He raises a brow as he gives me a long, meaningful look that tells me everything I need to know.

Oh shit.

I am so screwed.

"She was driving like a grandma and I was in a rush to get coffee home to Michelle," he explains to Calvin, and wait just one hot second.

Who the hell is Michelle?

I vaguely remember Calvin mentioning the man in my charge has a fiancée and a kid...

"I was driving like a normal person and he cut me off," I protest.

"You should've seen her try to tell me off when she walked in." He laughs at the memory. "So what are you doing here?" he asks.

"Mr. Bennett has hired me to—"

He cuts me off. "Wait a minute. You're telling me *you* are my babysitter?"

"Behavioral coach," Calvin and I say at the same time, though my voice holds a touch more exasperation than Calvin's.

"No." He shakes his head. "Wait." He holds up a hand. "*Hell* no."

"You don't have a choice, Mr. Dalton," Calvin reminds him.

"I don't just let anyone into my inner circle," he says.

Calvin sighs. "If you want to play next season, you need to be on your best behavior. Kathryn is here to help ensure you do that."

"Or you'll bench me?" Jack guesses, and he's totally pushing Calvin's buttons on purpose.

"You bet your ass I will," Calvin booms. "We have standards here, Dalton, and if you can't meet them, you won't play. Understand?"

Jack doesn't falter for even a second. "Yeah, I got it. Can I go now?"

"No," Calvin says. "Kathryn, have a seat. I'm going to go over the expectations, and once you're finished asking questions, you'll be free to go."

Calvin launches into every single detail from my contract (barring what he's paying me), and Jack pays exactly zero attention to him as he talks. Instead, he keeps glancing over at me, and when I feel his eyes on me and turn toward him, he looks away.

It's a pattern that happens over and over again, something that's already beyond frustrating. I feel like he wants to say something to me but obviously he isn't going to do it in front of Calvin.

Once Calvin wraps up the contract discussion and expectations, he pushes some papers across the desk. "This is the nondisclosure agreement Kathryn has already signed," he tells Jack. "I want you to review it and sign it. It's up to you, Jack, whether you want to admit the real reason Kathryn will be with you at all times or if you want to craft a reason for the media. I haven't told a soul about this arrangement barring Charles, my lawyer who drew up the contract. I understand the personal implications that might come along with a new woman tailing you everywhere you go, so I'm giving you the discretion of explaining her presence."

"Gee, thanks, boss," Jack says sarcastically. "Can we just say she's my side chick?"

God, I hate him.

Can I get a behavior coach, too? Because I might just throttle my client before this contract is up.

How do I babysit someone I can't stand for the next ten months?

A quarter of a million dollars, a little voice whispers in my head.

Right.

I can *totally* do this.

Maybe.

CHAPTER 10

It's absolutely shocking (in no way at all) that Jack drives like a maniac as I try to follow him back to the house where I'll be living for the next ten months. Thank God Lily texted me the address, because he loses me pretty much right away and I'm forced to rely on the GPS. Going forward, apparently I'll need to either drive him where he needs to go or be in the car with him when we're going somewhere.

I pick option one. I do value my life, after all.

I turn into the gated community and punch the gate code Lily sent into the little lockbox. The gate opens and I navigate through a neighborhood filled with mansions toward the one I'll be living in. I spot a nice view of Las Vegas Boulevard just twenty minutes down the road as I come up over a hill, and then my GPS tells me I have arrived.

I turn in and find another gate, and I press a button on one of the two openers Calvin handed me. This one opens the gate, and the other opens the garage. I'm not sure if I should park in the garage and just walk into the house or park in the driveway and use the front door the first time. It's not like they aren't expecting me, but still—it feels awkward to just barge in.

I don't even know where to bring my very out of place Kia to a stop in the long driveway. I creep up toward the front door and put it in park. There are plenty of other things to stress over that don't include a freaking driveway parking space.

I get out of the car and stare at the front of the house for a beat. I draw in a deep breath as I take in the splendor of this home...this *mansion*. Palm trees line the fancy entry that guests typically would use, and I have to remind myself that I'm not a guest here.

This is *home* now.

I walk up to the front door and knock a few times, but nobody comes to answer.

I knock a little louder.

Still nothing.

I try the bell.

A minute later, Jack appears. How freaking fast did he drive to not only arrive before me, but to be inside the house with the garage door already closed?

"For Christ's sake, Kia, don't you know you're not supposed to ring a doorbell at a house with a baby inside?" he says in greeting.

My eyes widen and I cover my mouth with my hand. He's grumpy, but I *did* just ring the doorbell and maybe they just got their baby down for a nap and oh shit this not a good way to start my first day here. "Oh my gosh, I am *so* sorry. I didn't realize—"

"Of course you didn't," some woman says curtly as she appears behind him. She's glamorous and gorgeous with a long curtain of dark hair and flashing dark eyes. She's wearing a low-cut, tight black shirt that shows off her slim figure paired with leggings that show off her tiny ass.

My immediate first impression is that she gives off this air like she's better than everybody else and I should feel privileged to share space in the same vicinity as her. I'm not quite convinced of that just yet. "Thank God Brooke's up there with JJ now."

Brooke?

JJ?

What the hell have I gotten myself into?

An older woman with silver feathered hair and a warm smile appears behind the glamorous woman. "You must be Kathryn," she says, and clearly these people were expecting me but I have no idea what Jack told them about why I'm actually here.

"Just call her *Kia*," Jack says, and I shoot him a glare.

"It's Kate, actually," I correct him, and he just smirks at me.

"I'm sure Jack and Michelle have already given you a warm welcome, but I'd also like to welcome you aboard. I'm Brenda, and I'm around a few times a week to cook and clean. If you need anything at all, just put it on the grocery list on the clipboard in the laundry room."

"And don't touch my orange Gatorade," Jack says.

"Or my Diet Pepsi," the woman I assume is Michelle says.

"Nice to meet you, Brenda." I offer a small smile and glance at Jack. "I'm more of a Coke kinda gal anyway," I say.

Brenda laughs, Jack huffs, and Michelle narrows her eyes.

"We haven't been formally introduced," I say to Michelle, sticking out my hand in a friendly hey let's shake on it since we're going to be living together sort of way. "I'm Kate."

"Mm," she says, pursing her lips, and then she spins and walks out of the room. It's in that moment that it hits me.

Was this the girlfriend he kicked me out for after he screwed me on a couch in a nightclub?

Does she somehow recognize me? Did Jack tell her about us? Is that why she was just so rude to me?

Jack leaves the room in the opposite direction from her, and then it's just Brenda and me standing in entryway as I clutch my laptop bag, my purse, and one of my overnight bags. "Let me show you around," she says. We head upstairs and past the first two rooms, which Brenda points out as the baby's nursery and Brooke's room. She shows me my room, too, where I drop my bags, along with additional bedrooms that separate our side of the house from the master suite. Brenda nods toward them but doesn't take me in.

The house has a total of seven bedrooms and eleven bathrooms. I want to stay and explore my bedroom with attached bathroom and walk-in closet, but I'm sure I'll have time later.

She continues the tour around the first floor where we see a movie room, a library, two offices—presumably a *his* and a *hers*, a dining room with an interesting full-sized wine refrigerator, a massive kitchen, a formal living room, a family room, and about a million other rooms.

According to Brenda, in the interest of full disclosure she points out where video cameras are located in each room and lets me know which are for security and which are for the baby monitor, not that I'll ever remember.

We step outside into a backyard oasis with a pool, waterslides, waterfalls, and palm trees along with a full-sized basketball court and an entire two-bedroom guest house that's bigger than my parents' house in Kansas. Landscape lights line walking paths all around the yard, and there's enough space back here to take a walk without ever having to leave the grounds.

I can't decide if that's amazing or a tad bit institutional.

Brenda is kind if a tad on the gossipy side, but it'll be nice to see at least one friendly face around here a few times a week. She fills me in on the basics, and I quickly learn that JJ, or Jack Alexander Dalton Junior, is the son Jack shares with Michelle, Brooke is the nanny, Michelle used to date Jack's brother, and Jack's brother used to be married to another of Jack's exes.

It's quite the little spider web.

She doesn't comment on the actual state of their relationship, but if Jack was screwing girls in nightclubs as little as five months ago, I definitely have some questions.

It's when we're outside away from all those video monitors that she spills a bit of tea. "Between the two of us, Michelle can be a handful, but so can Jack. You get two personalities like theirs together and you're bound to see some fireworks. But Calvin is intent on keeping his daughter happy. He wants to ensure his daughter is with the right man and that his grandson has a father he can look up to. I think that's why he brought Jack in from Denver. And I really think Jack has potential—in fact, he's a wonderful father to that sweet four-month-old boy, but he's just gotten a little off course lately. It probably has to do with his father." She whispers that last part a little dramatically, and I have no idea what went down with his father.

And also...she mentioned Calvin's daughter twice in that little spiel.

Who the hell is Calvin's daughter?

"Calvin's daughter?" I ask, using that as the starting point to the millions of questions her words raised.

Her brows dip a little. "Oh, you don't know? His daughter is Michelle."

Michelle?

Michelle-Michelle, like as in the rude lady inside who's engaged to Jack?

So let me get this straight.

I'm working with a man I had a tryst with on a couch in a nightclub who kicked me out when his apparently pregnant girlfriend showed up after someone snapped a photo of us that turned into a viral meme, and now I get to live with him and his evil fiancée and his four-month-old baby and shadow him everywhere he goes while said evil fiancée's father pays me a quarter of a million dollars over the next ten months?

Well that's a twist I didn't see coming.

CHAPTER 11

Brenda opens the slider door, and I follow her in.

I hear him before I see him...but when I see him, my eyes practically pop out of my head.

"Brenda, where's my orange Gatorade?" he asks.

He's wearing just a towel and a smirk.

Just.

A.

Towel.

And a smirk.

It's overwhelming. *He* is overwhelming. His freaking *abs* are overwhelming.

"There's more in the fridge in the laundry room," Brenda says, like seeing Jack Dalton wearing nothing but a towel is an everyday occurrence.

We had sex.

That man right there, the one asking about the orange Gatorade as he just stands there in a towel with all those abs everywhere, screwed me on a nightclub couch.

He's watching me. I *know* he is, and his abs flex a little. I can't stop staring, and his smirk turns into a laugh. "You need anything, Kia?"

"It's *Kate*," I grit out, and I hate him and how he can so easily read me. I'm the one here to get inside *his* head, not the other way around.

He stalks out of the room to grab his drink from the other fridge, and I settle in at the kitchen table with my phone while I wait around to see what my next job responsibility is going to be.

A short while later, I hear Jack coming down the stairs, his voice carrying through the house. Brenda's already gone for the day and Brooke is occupied with JJ, so I've just been hanging around by myself on my first day as I wait to see what's up next.

"Hey Tom."

"It's official," the voice on the other end of his speakerphone says. "You're the newest quarterback of the Vegas Aces."

Jack is quiet at that news.

"Congratulations, Jack," Tom says.

"Thanks," he says, and he stalks into the kitchen. His eyes fall onto me. "You know Bennett hired me a babysitter?"

"Good," Tom says. "You probably need one."

"I'm a grown-ass man," he says, his eyes on me as he talks. "I know how to take care of myself."

"Clearly you don't, Jack. Did you really think going to a strip club with Ben Olson the night before the trade was made official was a smart move?"

I raise a pointed brow in his direction. I like whoever this Tom guy is.

Jack laughs. "Smart or not, we had a hell of a lot of fun. Besides, the paperwork is filed. It must've solidified Zimmer's decision to get rid of me, so mission accomplished."

"What will you tell people?" he asks.

"What do you mean?" Jack tilts his head as his eyes shift out the window.

"I mean people are going to want to know who she is when they see some new chick tailing you everywhere. The press already knows you're engaged to Michelle, so you can't fake a relationship with her."

He laughs. "That's more my brother's MO."

His brother faked a relationship? That's an interesting tidbit I tuck away for later.

"I thought maybe it ran in the family," Tom says lightly.

Jack's eyes move back to mine and he raises a brow. "I'll think of something."

Tom blows out a breath. "Just try to behave yourself, all right?"

"Eh, we'll see." He cuts the call and slides into the chair across from me. He sighs.

"I'm going to need access to your calendar," I jump in before he can start up the conversation about how we're going to lie away my position here.

"Nah, I'm good," he says, and he's so freaking arrogant. "You have access to whatever Cal gave you, so that should be good enough."

"It's not." My nostrils flare as I force myself to remain professional. Calvin didn't give me access to *anything*, so I have no idea what's on his agenda—even when it's Aces-related. "My job is to stay on top of you at all times, not just for Aces events."

He raises a brow. "Stay on top of me?" He leans in and lowers his voice so it's all raspy and husky. "You mean like you did in a private suite of a nightclub last Halloween?"

My eyes widen and my cheeks burn with mortification. "You remember?" I squeak.

"Of course I do." His eyes lock on mine for a beat, but then he seems to think better of it. He shakes his head. "You look different than that night."

The gruffness of his voice presses an ache between my thighs.

Shit.

"I cut my hair."

"I can see that." He nods and narrows his eyes. "But why?"

He's teetering on the edge of something unprofessional, something that's the opposite of what I've been brought in to do. I change the subject as quickly as I can. "Let's just put it behind us."

"I think we should at least address it."

"Really?" I ask. "You *really* want to do this right now?"

He glances over his shoulder, which tells me Michelle must be around somewhere. He shrugs. "Yeah, I really want to do this."

"Okay then. I thought we were having a nice time on Halloween, and then you kicked me out because your *girlfriend* showed up. What kind of asshole screws a girl on a couch when he has a girlfriend?"

"So you cut your hair?" he presses, ignoring the baring of my very soul.

I stare down at the table. "Every time I saw that meme, which was *everywhere* right after it happened...hell, *you* were everywhere...you *are* everywhere—and every single time, I was reminded of what a douchebag you are. I chopped my hair off for a fresh start." I finally lift my eyes to his. "You and my best friend are the only two people in the world who know the real identity of the cat burglar, and it will stay that way for the rest of time."

He sighs. "She wasn't really my girlfriend at the time."

My brows dip. "What?" I'm quite sure I didn't hear him correctly. It was such a defining moment in my history, and to hear that it wasn't what I thought it was plows into my stomach like a ton of bricks.

"We weren't together, not *really*, but I didn't know what else to call her. She was seven months pregnant with my kid. It was just a strange situation, and I panicked."

"*You* panicked?" I ask, shocked by that revelation. I think of the defensive linemen plowing their way toward him every Sunday. He's always so controlled and precise. Panic just doesn't seem to be a part of his vocabulary. "But you're not the panicking type."

"On the field, no, I'm not. But sometimes..." He blows out a breath. "*Fuck*. I know this is five months too late, but when you and I met, my father had just died, and about a month before that, I found out Michelle was carrying my kid. Michelle and I were never serious. We slept together once in a while. She was in love with my brother. When I learned the baby was mine, I made some poor choices."

"Poor choices? Like me?" I guess, clearly affected most by those words despite the other revelations he just admitted.

"That's not what I meant," he says softly.

"I found out my boyfriend had been cheating on me about a week before Halloween. And then we had our thing, and you had a girlfriend. You were as big a piece of shit in my eyes as my cheating ex was."

I leave out the whole thing about how he stomped on my already beaten down self-worth and how I haven't been able to *really* date anybody since those two things happened back-to-back. I leave out the part about how I'm damaged now in part because of what he did. To be honest, he just added more shit on top of the shit sundae Blake left behind. It wasn't *totally* his fault, but he certainly didn't help. And then I made a fool out of myself in front of Vince, and I think it's fair to say I'm not jumping into any dating pools any time soon.

His gaze drops to the counter. "I was in a bad place. I did things I shouldn't have, and I'm sorry you got caught in that. I'm sorry I hurt you. And after those poor choices, excluding you, I ultimately decided to give it a try with her for JJ's sake."

"And that's where you're at now?" I guess.

"At the corner of whatever you'd call that and regret," he mutters just loudly enough for me to hear.

My chest tightens. "What are you saying?"

"Nothing." He shakes his head, and the sharp, stormy look in his eyes tells me this conversation is over.

That's all he's going to give me.

For now.

I never really expected I'd ever run into Jack Dalton again after that night. What are the chances of a regular girl like me running into the same celebrity twice in a lifetime, let alone a third time? But I assumed that if I ever *did* see him again, all I'd feel is hate.

That's not what this is.

Yeah, I hate him. But I'm also inappropriately attracted to him. It's not just an attraction. It's visceral. It's imprinted on my soul.

It doesn't matter. I'm working with him now, and he's engaged to another woman, and there are lots of lines here that would be wrong to cross for both of us.

It'd be my own ass on the line if I acted on that attraction.

Of course he remembers that night.

Of course this is just going to get more and more awkward.

Of course I can't stop thinking about what it felt like to kiss him.

A quarter of a million dollars.

Owning my own interior design firm.

Building the life I want for myself.

If I do anything to mess this up, I'm losing my chance at everything I've wanted for my future.

I can do this.

I'm locked in. I'm the degreed professional in psychology, and yet I can't seem to figure out how to act. I guess just because we've studied a certain field doesn't automatically mean we're destined to behave a certain way.

"So can I have access to your calendar?" I ask quietly.

"No. I said it back in Cal's office, and I'll say it again. I don't just let anybody into my inner circle. I'll let you know my schedule."

"Fine," I mutter. But that's twice now he's mentioned his inner circle, and I can't help but wonder who, exactly, makes up that circle.

He glances over his shoulder and lowers his voice again. "You know I still get meowed at everywhere I go?"

I can't help a soft giggle.

He raises a brow. "You think that's funny?"

I lift a shoulder. "You see why I cut my hair now?"

He chuckles, but before he gets a chance to respond, Michelle strolls in. She leaps over to Jack and tosses her arms around his neck before she plants a kiss on his cheek.

I catch the look on Jack's face before he smooths it over.

He doesn't want her arms around him...but *she* is in that circle.

Why?

"Hey sweetie." Her voice is all syrupy sweet and I want to gag. "I'm heading out with Savannah and Krista. Do I look okay?"

"You're going out with *Savannah*?" he asks, ignoring her question.

She looks gorgeous, though my personal choice for a night out with girlfriends wouldn't be a revealing dress with heels six inches tall, but I guess I prefer comfort over style most of the time.

And also...who's Savannah?

"Yeah. We're talking football wife stuff. Is that a problem?" Her tone is innocent, but something about her facial expression tells me she's anything but.

"No," he says, and his voice is a clear contradiction to his single word. "But she's not going to be a wife much longer." He smirks. "Have fun."

"You know I will." She smiles sweetly at him and catches his lips with hers. He pulls back quickly, and it could be because they're in front of me—the newest employee living in their home, or perhaps he's sparing me their affection since we once slept together, or maybe, just *maybe*, he doesn't want to be kissing her at all.

My brain tells me it's the first reason or maybe the second, but my stupid heart is hoping it's the third.

I continue to analyze their interaction even after she has bolted out the door. Not only do I have questions about Savannah, Krista, and football wife stuff, but this Michelle chick is something else, too.

She never even *looked* at me. I'm nothing to her, just someone on daddy's payroll. She smothered him with affection in front of me to stake her claim on him.

And *that* is the root of it all. I know nothing about Jack Dalton, not really, other than the fact that he's engaged to Michelle and they share a child. But my analytical mind is already piecing together that he doesn't want to be with her, and I can't help but wonder why he is.

He could be with any woman he wants. Why is he marrying her?

Calvin is paying me to help him make good decisions.

Is marrying her a good decision?

Or is he doing it to keep his new team owner happy?

These are all questions I want the answers to, and not just because I'm attracted to him. It's because that's what I'm being paid to do.

But I have a sneaking suspicion that getting Jack to dump Michelle is the last thing Calvin would deem *good behavior*.

I've only been on the job a few hours, and I'm already having moral dilemmas.

"It hit the media," he says quietly as he stares down at his phone.

"What did?"

"The trade." He presses his lips together as he scans something on his phone.

"Is that good news?"

He lifts a shoulder. "I knew it was coming. It just makes it official, and it means my phone's about to start ringing and I have to put on the act, you know?"

"The act?" I press. I'm surprised he's telling *me* this. Isn't this a conversation he should be having with his fiancée? Maybe not since her dad owns the team.

"Like this is what I want." He says the words flatly.

"You don't want to be here?"

His eyes lift from his phone to me. "You think I want my future father-in-law to have this sort of control over my life? You think I want a fucking babysitter? No offense, Kia. I'm sure you're great, but this wouldn't have happened if literally *any* other team in the league picked me up." He shakes his head and stands as his eyes return to his phone. "It had to be the goddamn Aces."

"It's Kate," I grit out.

He ignores me and picks up a call with an enthusiasm I haven't heard from him before. "Hey, Dean!" His demeanor flips in an instant from the truth under what he just told me to the persona he clearly puts on for the media.

He heads toward his office, and I'm not quite sure how much I'm supposed to shadow him, but I figure he wants to be alone in there. Hearing his cheerful *Hey, Dean* tells me he's handling at least this part of his life with professionalism.

Now if I could just get him to handle the rest with the same attitude, it'll be an easy, breezy path to two hundred fifty grand.

CHAPTER 12

I get to know Brooke a bit while JJ naps and Jack fields calls about the trade, and I find she's a twenty-one-year-old student studying elementary education at UNLV. She attends classes part-time while JJ is in daycare during the mornings, and we spend over an hour discussing her coursework and professors—some the very same ones I had when I attended the same school.

She has a long-term boyfriend of several years who's studying to be a lawyer, and his cousin is Calvin's assistant, Lily. That whole chain is how she ended up in the position of JJ's nanny. She seems really sweet, like we could have some nice chats. Since she's an employee bound by the same nondisclosure agreement I signed with my contract, I wonder whether we can chat about what I'm *really* doing here, but I want to clear it with Jack first...so for now, I keep it vague.

She heads upstairs to get JJ when he starts making a little noise through the monitor, and she brings him down a few minutes later.

It's my first time meeting Jack's baby boy, and I swoon.

He's the cutest little boy I've ever seen.

He has rosy cheeks, a smattering of dark blond hair that hasn't quite grown in yet, and eyes the same shade of navy as his daddy's. There's no mistaking he's Jack's son.

"You want to hold him?" she asks.

I nod and take him gently from her, protecting his sweet little head as I do, and I feel a twinge in my chest. I loved nannying for Kennedy in the two months I was there before Miles was born, but it was when the baby came along that I really started to enjoy my job. It just made me realize how very much I want kids of my own someday.

Holding this little boy makes me feel those same things all over again. I'm only twenty-five, so I've got plenty of time, but I grew up as an only child. I want a kid, and I want siblings for that kid.

Right now, and for approximately the next year, I have zero prospects in the way of actually making that happen. Unless I happen to meet one of Jack's hot football buddies. Then maybe.

Yeah, right.

But that Ben Olson guy isn't hard to look at...

When Jack eventually emerges from his office, he looks worn down. He heads right for the pantry and grabs a bottle of gin off the top shelf, and he sets it on the counter. That's when he glances up and spots me holding JJ.

He abandons the bottle on the counter and makes his way toward us. "May I?" he asks, holding out his hands to indicate he wants to hold his baby. I hand him over, and he looks down at JJ.

"Did you sleep good, little buddy?" he croons softly.

And I swoon. Again.

Jeez.

He stares down at him with all the love in the world, enough to make my eyes prick with a little heat. He's this big, tough, condescending, egotistical asshole, and yet seeing him just look down at his son the way he is makes him almost...human.

Almost sweet.

Almost, but not quite.

He opens the slider doors and takes the baby outside, and I glance at Brooke.

"He's *so good* with JJ," she says.

I think about asking whether Michelle is good with her son, but before I get a chance to ask, she starts talking.

"They're an interesting couple." She walks over to the window to watch Jack with the baby in her charge. "But they share a child, so I guess they're trying to make it work."

I stand beside her, and we both watch Jack as he walks around the yard talking to his son. "How long have you been nannying for them?"

"Since JJ was born, so right about four months." She seems like she wants to add more, but she also doesn't know me well enough to trust me yet. "Just look at him," she says, and we both do.

My eyes drift down from his torso to his narrow hips to his butt, and I sigh.

Reality check, Kate.

We're looking at the baby, not at Jack's ass.

"He really tries so hard to be a good dad, and he does a great job. But with him going back and forth to Denver and working so much even when he's here, I get why he wants me around to be that constant in his son's life."

"What about Michelle?" I ask.

She clears her throat, and she's quiet a while before she finally answers. "I've heard horror stories of mothers who hated their nannies because they felt like the nanny had a stronger bond with the child, so I actively look for places to include her in our daily routine. But every single time I've asked, she's had something else she needs to do." She lifts a shoulder and glances over at me. "She tries, too," she scrambles to say, which just tells me she's trying to cover the fact that she's gossiping about her boss regardless of what she actually believes. "But she's just so busy with her circle of friends and her job."

"What does she do?"

"She works with the Aces as an assistant to the marketing director, but she wants to assist her father instead. He already has two assistants, and he calls on her upon occasion when he needs additional help."

"Her father?" I repeat.

She nods. "They're super close." She twists her middle finger over her pointer finger. "Two peas in a pod."

Jack walks back toward us, so that's the end of our conversation. But it's interesting to note that Michelle and her dad are as close as Brooke claims they are, and I can't help but wonder whether that has something to do with why I have a job here.

Once Brooke gets JJ going on his bottle, Jack glances over at me. "Can we talk in my office?"

"Of course," I say, and I ignore the racing in my chest. Why do I have the sudden feeling like I'm in trouble?

I follow him to the office, and I slide into the chair across from him.

It's leather and plush at the same time, like I could sit here all day and not get a stiff back.

"Who are you and why are you here?" Jack asks.

My brows draw together. "I'm Kate and your new team owner hired me as a different sort of coach for you."

He picks up a pen and flips it around between his fingers. "Yeah, no shit. That's not what I meant. What are we telling the media when they ask who you are since you'll be blessing my public presence at all times?"

I stare at him blankly. Calvin had mentioned we should have a plan, and with the whirlwind today has been, I sort of forgot.

"The look on your face clearly tells me you haven't given it any thought. It doesn't take very long in the spotlight to realize you *always* need to be prepared."

"Got it. You know you *can* talk to me without being condescending *all* the time," I say, my voice full of sugar.

He ignores me and continues thinking aloud. "We can't say you're my girlfriend since I'm engaged to Michelle."

"Uh, is there something wrong with *the truth*?" I ask.

He gives me a look like I'm stupid, and it's not the first time I've had the urge to slap him. My fingers flex in my lap where they rest.

He never stops flipping the pen, and my eyes fall to it as I just sit back and observe for a beat.

"Yes," he says.

"What?"

He blows out an exasperated breath. "I can't tell people I have an adult babysitter. It's ridiculous."

"And yet it's your reality." I smile sweetly. If he's going to patronize me, I'm going to push his buttons right back.

He's deep in thought as he flips that damn pen around some more, and when he glances up at me, he catches me watching. His brows dip as he stops and sets the pen down.

He knows what I'm going to say.

It's a nervous tick from a man who is *never* nervous, at least not on the outside. He's showing me an insecurity as he deals with this new reality, and the last thing he would possibly want is for a stranger outside his inner circle to observe any sort of vulnerability on his part.

But it's my job to pull those things out of him even though I already know he's going to fight me every step of the way.

"It's okay to keep doing that," I say gently. "It's the first time you've let your guard down."

"And that's why I stopped," he says pointedly.

"We'll say I'm a friend," I suggest.

He shakes his head. "Not good enough."

"Manager? Agent? Publicist?" I toss out different ideas to see what will stick.

"My current manager, agent, and publicist might have something to say about that."

I look up at the ceiling and tap my chin as I think, my lips twisting as I squint. And then I snap my fingers as it comes to me. "Got it. I'm your new assistant."

He tilts his head and narrows his eyes as he studies me for a beat, and then he nods. "That could work."

My brows shoot up in total shock that he actually approves of my idea. "Holy cheeseballs. Really?"

"Cheeseballs?" he repeats, his tone definitely mocking.

"I worked with children at my last position. I sort of got used to screening my language. But really, you think the assistant thing could work?"

He shrugs. "Sure. I just need to make sure the people who know don't say anything."

"Does Michelle know?" I ask.

He shakes his head, and truthfully I'm shocked by that. Shouldn't his fiancée-slash-the daughter of the guy who made this whole deal happen know the truth?

"What did her dad tell her?" I ask.

"He just said you're a type of coach, and she doesn't really give a shit. I'll talk to Tom and Ben, though, because they know. And my family."

"Tom and Ben?" I ask.

"Tom's my agent. And Ben Olson," he says. "An old friend who was also recently traded to the Aces."

"The one you went to the strip club with last night?" I ask.

He purses his lips and shakes his head with a bit of disgust. "See? I can't do a goddamn thing without the entire world finding out."

"Well it *was* another mark against you. You have a fiancée and a baby at home and you're out drinking at a strip club. Do you really not see at all how that's problematic?"

He flattens his lips. "I don't need to answer to anybody."

"Except your boss," I point out. "Your future father-in-law. God, how stuck must you feel right now?" I'm pushing here, and I say the last part rhetorically.

I'm shocked when he answers anyway.

"Incredibly."

My eyes flash to his, and he looks away before I get the chance to read what he's thinking. "Then why are you marrying her?"

"Long story." He clears his throat. "I have a few more things to do including preparing for a press conference welcoming me to the team tomorrow, and then I'm meeting some people for dinner."

"Where are we going?" I ask. When he frowns at me, I add, "I just want to know how I should dress."

His frown deepens. "You can wear whatever you want in the house, though I'd keep it PG at the worst since there's a baby. Not that his mother does." He says that last part under his breath.

"Cute, Jack, but I'm coming with you." I purse my lips at him.

"The fuck you are."

"Might I remind you that your boss is paying me to be there, so yes, in fact, I certainly am." I cross my arms over my chest and drum my fingers on my bicep as my heart races at standing up to him.

His eyes fall to my fingers where they move, and I realize I'm showing him my own nervous tick. I stop drumming immediately.

"Calling in the big guns on the first day?" he asks.

"Don't make this harder on both of us."

He sighs. "Fine. But you're not sitting at my table, and I'm not paying for your meal. And if for some reason my dinner companions acknowledge you, none of this *holy cheeseballs* ridiculousness."

I smile sweetly, but it's really just to mask my glare. "Yes, sir," I say, and I can't ignore the tiny bit of heat in his eyes at my submissive reply.

CHAPTER 13

I walk a few paces behind Jack as we enter the restaurant, and he walks toward a table near the back. It's not super crowded for a Monday night, which is nice given the fact that I'm here with a celebrity.

Sort of.

I'm not allowed at his table, so technically I'm not here with a celebrity. Technically I'm at the same restaurant as one.

He's being a dick, which I should have expected when I was hired for this position regardless of who my client turned out to be. He's thirty-three and used to doing whatever he wants, and now he has someone constantly breathing down his neck. I'm sure it's not fun, but I'm not being paid to be fun.

And when he slides into a booth across from two other people, one of which looks to be very pregnant, I see why he wasn't ready for me to sit at the table with them.

I'm a huge Vegas Aces fan, and the fact that Jack Dalton is sitting at the same table as Luke Dalton at a restaurant in Las Vegas the day the trade went public is definitely newsworthy.

The table they chose is far in the back, and there's nobody else sitting anywhere near it. The tall booth walls create plenty of privacy. Still, I choose the table closest theirs so I can keep an eye on Jack.

But somehow I doubt his brother and the pregnant woman beside him are going to talk him into a strip club.

A minute later, an older woman with a sharp, dark bob and shrewd blue eyes walks through the restaurant and slides into the booth beside Jack.

"Where's JJ?" she asks without a greeting, and I'm at the perfect distance to hear the entire conversation as long as they don't lower their voices.

"Home with Brooke," Jack says. He tosses an arm around her shoulder and leans in to kiss her cheek. "How've you been, Mom?"

Mom. So this is literally just a nice family dinner out. He could've told me that.

I guess it wouldn't have changed anything.

A girl who looks to be in her early twenties rushes through the restaurant, and I get a little nervous she's a fan as she approaches the table with two hot football players sitting at it. "Kay! You made it," the mom says, and I have no idea who *Kay* is but apparently she's part of this crew. She greets everyone as she squeezes in beside Jack and the mom.

"Luke said you have a babysitter now?" the mom asks, and my chest squeezes. They're talking about me. I'm just a short table away and they don't even know it. "Is that in addition to Brooke?"

"It's not for JJ," Luke says with far too much merriment.

"It's for Jack," the woman beside Luke says, her voice a little lower but still full of merriment as well.

"What?" the mom asks.

Jack blows out a breath, something I notice he does a lot. "It's not a babysitter." He doesn't try to hide his exasperation, but he lowers his voice so anyone who might be listening wouldn't be able to hear. I strain to catch what he says. "Cal hired a behavior coach."

I stare down at my menu even though I *so badly* want to see the mother's facial reaction to that news. "For what?" she asks.

"To keep me out of trouble," he mutters.

"That's not a bad thing, Jack," the mom says.

"Where is she now?" the woman next to Luke asks.

My heart starts racing as I realize I might actually meet Jack Dalton's entire family right now, including the brother I've watched every Sunday during the football season for the last decade...and it's not just that.

I've slept with Jack, and now I might be meeting his family. I realize these two things are completely unrelated. It's not like he's introducing me as his girlfriend. I'm *not* his girlfriend, nor do I want to be knowing the way he treats people.

And yet...he's been inside me.

I can't forget that night.

I can't forget the passion and the heat between us.

I can't forget what it felt like as he moved inside me and his eyes locked on mine.

Holy cheeseballs. Did it just get about a thousand degrees hotter in here?

I fan myself with my menu.

"She's right here. Kia!" Jack calls, and I glance up. He flicks his neck as if to tell me it's okay to come over to their table.

I close my eyes a beat as I wish away the redness in my cheeks, and then I turn around. "It's Kate, actually," I say with a little wave. "Nice to meet all of you."

The woman next to Luke motions with her hand in a *come on over* kind of way, and I glance at Jack, who looks annoyed but also a little defeated.

I stand and cross the few feet over toward their table, and the woman pats the booth beside her as she pushes in closer to Luke. "Come join us," she says. "I'm Ellie, Jack's sister-in-law."

Luke waves. "And I'm his brother, Luke."

"I know who you are," I say, and my cheeks redden even more. "I'm a huge fan."

Jack snorts across the table, and his mother smacks him in the arm in a *be nice* sort of way.

"It's nice to meet you," Luke says. "You are *exactly* what my big brother needs."

I chuckle. "He doesn't seem to think so."

I'm introduced to Kaylee, who is the Dalton sister, and the family asks me a little about my background and Jack quietly mentions how I'm his new assistant to everyone outside this little circle.

Aha! The circle again. This is part of it.

We order our dinners, and I can't help but appreciate the dynamic around this table.

Luke and Ellie are adorable together and seem like a whole lot of fun as they try to put Jack in his place. Jack's mother, Carol, is serious but seems to lighten up a little when her kids call her out. They chat for a bit about JJ, but nobody mentions their father.

I sit quietly and listen as Carol fills the boys in on everybody's lives from the town in Michigan where they grew up, and I learn that Carol recently moved from Michigan out here to Vegas, and she's absolutely thrilled that both her sons are in the same city for once. I discover that Kaylee will be moving in with Carol as soon as she graduates college in May. She already got a job at a middle school here in Vegas that'll start in a couple months. She'd thought about staying in Michigan, but with her entire family here in Vegas, making the move made sense.

Carol treats everyone to dinner, including me. When I offer to pay for my own, I'm met with a stern look that basically tells me to sit down. And so I do.

I'm ready to head home once the meal has been paid for, and it's only then I realize I don't get to make that call. I *won't* get to make that call for the next ten months. I'm at his mercy, and I suppose I should count myself lucky that his family was just so nice to me.

He catches my eye from across the table. "Anyone up for one more drink?" he asks, and I know he's not asking *me* if I want a drink when he smirks in my direction. He's waiting for me to tell him not to drink.

I don't care if he has a drink or two, or even three or four. What might come *after* those drinks is what I need to watch out for.

"We're good for one or two more," Luke says, his arm around Ellie's shoulders.

She nods and holds up her water. "I might get crazy and switch to Sprite, though."

"I'm going to head out," Carol says.

"She's my ride," Kaylee jokes. "I took an Uber here. And I have a meeting in the morning at the school."

Kaylee and Carol scoot out of the booth after Jack kisses his mom's cheek. Ellie and Luke bid their farewells, too. "Nice meeting you, Kate. Take good care of Jack," Carol says.

I offer a warm smile. "I will."

"Are we staying here?" Luke asks, and I stand and move across to the seat Carol and Kaylee just vacated. I'm beside Jack, but it felt weird staying on the same side with Luke and Ellie when Jack was over there by himself.

"We can start here," Jack says.

Ellie laughs and shakes her head. "Yep, a babysitter is a *fantastic* idea for you."

"How are you really handling all of it?" Luke asks. "The trade, Calvin, Michelle..."

Jack sighs and glances down at the table. "I'm handling it."

"Are you?" Luke asks. He glances at me and then back at Jack. "I assume she signed an NDA?"

Jack nods.

"I figured you would've broken off the engagement by now," Luke says as he lowers his voice. "Don't give me this bullshit that you're so in love with her because only a few months ago you said you had no idea how I put up with her, and then suddenly she has Grandma Rose's ring on her finger?"

Jack lowers his voice, too, and he leans forward a little to make sure the conversation is just for the four of us...or three of them, but I'm here, too. "It's the right thing to do. We share a child. And she gave me Grandma's ring back."

Ellie snorts with disgust.

"It has nothing to do with Dad's will?" Luke asks.

Jack presses his lips together but doesn't respond to that.

"What's she getting out of it?" Luke presses.

"The man she loves," Jack says.

Luke snorts. "Oh, please. She doesn't love anybody but herself."

"Ain't that the truth," Jack mutters.

"What about JJ?" I ask, mostly because my curiosity takes over.

All three heads at the table swing in my direction.

"Of course she loves her son," Ellie says softly.

"But *she* will always come first," Luke adds.

They both nod as they press their lips together like it's a tragedy. Jack seems to be doing what he can to be a good parent to his son, but I'm not so sure the same can be said for Michelle. I can't help but wonder whether *she* would benefit from a behavior coach, too.

Jack appears to be an adult who can fare fine without me, and the longer I sit at this table, the more I think Michelle's father brought him to the Aces and subsequently hired me as a way to keep a thumb on his future son-in-law.

So I'm faced with my second moral dilemma of my first day on the job.

Do I do anything about it? Or do I just shut my mouth and collect my paycheck?

As a psychologist, the welfare of my patient is supposed to be my top priority. But there are two issues at play with that: for one, my client is technically Calvin, not Jack. And second, am I technically practicing psychology when, let's face it, I'm nothing more than an adult babysitter?

As tainted as that money may be, when I think about my future without it...well, I don't think there's a real choice in the matter.

CHAPTER 14

The first day was a lot.

But I'm up to the task. I'm used to chasing toddlers. Chasing Jack isn't much different.

I can't pretend like meeting his family didn't affect me deeply. I enjoyed talking with them and getting to sit in Jack's inner circle even if it was only for a couple hours.

That's rather alarming.

We stayed at the same restaurant for one final drink before we headed home. I stayed up until Jack closed his door to go to bed, and I set my alarm for five in the morning so I could get up, shower, and attempt to get some schoolwork done before it all started over again.

Part of me wonders whether I need some sort of baby monitor. Is it okay for me to sleep? What if he sneaks out in the middle of the night?

These things are out of my control, and I can only do what is within my means.

I find myself distracted looking up articles about Jack Dalton when I *should* be doing my assignments in the morning.

I'm studying his history. I'm trying to figure him out little by little. But it's hard to separate fact from fiction on the internet, and I think I'd be better served by talking to the man himself.

But getting him to open up to me is a different story entirely.

On my second day, I ride in Jack's truck with him to the practice facility for a press conference. I grip my purse so tightly my knuckles turn white as he weaves in and out of traffic the whole way there, and I'm terrified for my life. I send up a prayer of gratitude when we finally pull into a parking space.

The ride is over.

We made it.

"You can stop using your invisible passenger side brake now," he says.

I glance down, and my right foot is jammed against the floor in such a way that makes it appear as though I'm stepping on a brake. I hadn't even realized I was doing it. "Your driving is terrifying."

He laughs. "You're easy to scare," he says.

Ain't that the truth.

We head inside, and I follow Jack through some hallways and into a big room with a bunch of chairs facing a small stage. On the stage is a table with microphones in front of it and two chairs behind it. A backdrop with the Aces logo on repeat over and over perches behind the table, and video cameras are set up in various key places including directly in front of the table.

"Jack," Calvin says with a broad smile. "So glad you're here. Let's head to the locker room."

We follow Calvin through the press conference room and into a locker room, and he takes Jack over to a cubby with a bench and some cabinets above it along with a pole to hang clothes on. An Aces jersey with *DALTON 5* on it hangs on display on that pole.

"Welcome to the Aces," Calvin says. "This is your locker. The press is arriving any minute, and they'll start asking their questions in thirty minutes. Take some time to get acclimated, look around the locker room, talk to your agent or publicist if you need to, and prepare yourself however you do for a press conference."

"Yes, sir," Jack says. He stares at the jersey, and in fact I haven't seen him look away from it since we both first spotted it.

"Can I get you anything?" he asks.

Jack shakes his head.

"Mitch and Steve will be by shortly," Calvin says, and he presses his lips together and nods at me before he exits the locker room.

"Who are Mitch and Steve?" I ask.

"Mitch Thompson is the head coach," he says. "Steve Shanahan is the general manager." He's still staring at the jersey.

"Do you need to call your agent or publicist?" I ask, simply repeating what Calvin just mentioned.

"No," he murmurs.

I stand quietly beside him, not really sure what he's staring at. He shakes his head and seems to snap out of it. "Are you okay?"

"Yeah." He blows out a breath. "Just the first time I'm seeing an Aces jersey with my last name and *my* number on it...not Luke's."

"Is it surreal?"

He nods. "Incredibly."

He seems almost...human today.

The coach and general manager come in and introduce themselves, and I see him switch from the introspective man staring at his jersey who seemed like he was on the precipice of opening up to me into the charismatic athlete everybody loves both on and off the field.

I watch him during the press conference as he thanks Mitch, Steve, and the entire Bennett family for the opportunity, and I listen to his words as he talks about learning his new roles and responsibilities with this team. I watch as he talks animatedly and excitedly about the potential to bring more wins to Vegas, about meeting his new teammates and setting goals with them. I watch as he fields questions like an absolute pro—even though he didn't talk to his agent *or* his publicist immediately before the questions began. He addresses what it'll be like to play with his brother here in Vegas, too, and how excited he is to get started.

He was human for a minute with me, but then he turned back into the professional he's known as. I just hope I get more opportunities to glimpse the man he was if for only a few seconds with me.

I think he's someone I could actually grow to like.

CHAPTER 15

"Good morning, JD-Five," I say brightly from my spot at the kitchen table as Jack saunters in after his workout. He's in mesh shorts and he isn't wearing a shirt and *God* this job is really great sometimes. "What's on the agenda for the day?" I figure it's an easy door to open conversation, so I'm making it my morning mantra when I first see Jack...especially since I don't have access to his calendar.

"A few of my buddies are coming over this afternoon," he says. "And I approve of the new nickname."

I laugh. "What's the plan?"

"Drunk cornhole." He says it so nonchalantly, like it's just what guys do when they get together. "Maybe poker. Maybe cigars, but I'm not really a cigar guy."

"Ugh," Michelle says as she sweeps into the room. "No cigars."

"Definitely cigars," Jack mutters.

She wrinkles her nose. "You'll smell like Daddy."

Jack grins and winks at me. "Then I can use that whole *who's your daddy* line."

Michelle smacks him in the arm lightly, and he just laughs. It's the first time I've seen any sort of affectionate interaction between the two of them, and it still boils down to Michelle whining about something.

"I'm working on a project with the marketing team and I have dinner and drinks with Natalie later, so I'll be home late," Michelle says.

"Great." Jack almost seems like he means it—his single word doesn't come across as sarcastic but rather a little thankful that she won't be around the entire day. I chalk it up to the fact that he's having friends over and he doesn't really want his fiancée at drunken cornhole with his buddies.

He probably doesn't want *me* there, either, but he doesn't have much choice in that particular matter.

Michelle leaves and Brooke takes JJ to a playdate for a few hours, which leaves Jack and me alone at the house. He takes a shower, and when he comes down, that sexy and masculine Jack scent seems to follow him.

I try my hardest not to breathe it in.

I don't even really like this guy, and yet I do. It's so damn confusing.

A little after lunchtime, his *buddies* start arriving. Up first is Jack's brother Luke who arrives with another Aces player I recognize as wide receiver Josh Nolan.

"This is my new assistant, Kia," Jack says to Josh. I shoot Jack a quick glare.

"Nice to meet you, Kia," Josh says, sticking out his hand.

"It's, uh, Kate, actually."

"It's still nice to meet you, *uh Kate actually*," Josh teases.

I laugh. "Nice to meet you, too."

"She's the babysitter," Luke says to Josh.

Jack turns swiftly in his direction. "You told him?"

Luke shrugs. "It was too damn funny not to. Don't worry, we can trust Josh."

"I know we can, but the more people who know, the more likely our secret is to get out."

"It's more fun this way," Luke says.

The bell rings, and Jack opens it to the tight end I recognize as the very attractive Ben Olson. The party of four hot men (plus me) is complete.

"Ben, this is Kia, my assistant," Jack says.

"Is that what we're calling her?" Ben asks with an easy laugh, and my cheeks turn a shade of red.

Jack leans in toward me. "Ben and I go way back. I confessed to him the night before I met you that Calvin had hired me a babysitter."

He'd already mentioned that to me when we came up with our lie about being his assistant, but I wonder how many other people know that little tidbit. It's good to know Ben is a person Jack considers part of his inner circle...and apparently his brother and Josh, too. Not that he had a choice on Josh, I guess.

"I'm Kate," I say, sticking out my hand.

"Nice to meet you," Ben says, and he brings the back of my hand to his lips. I can't tell if he's being serious or facetious but my cheeks heat at the feel of his lips on my skin.

Jack's off the market, but it seems as though the very sexy Ben might be up for grabs.

Jack glares at Ben before he leads the group of men through the house and into the backyard. I hang toward the back of the pack as the feeling that today's going to be a long day washes over me.

Jack has already set up cornhole boards themed to the Vegas Aces, tape for the foul lines and pitchers' boxes, and a cooler in the backyard. They all reach into the cooler and pop open a beer before they get started.

"I'll be fine out here," Jack says to me in some attempt to dismiss me.

"Oh, no," Ben says. "The *assistant* stays, and the three of us are going to put her to the test today."

I narrow my eyes at him, not sure exactly what he means by that.

"How?" Jack asks for me.

"If her job is to stop you from making an ass of yourself, we'll find ways to get you to make an ass of yourself," Ben says. "What was it...headlines and handcuffs? You think we could get you into both today?"

I picture Jack in handcuffs for the briefest second. Not the kind where he's being arrested, but the kind where he's tied down and I can do whatever I want to him.

I can think of a few things.

I shake the thoughts right out of my head. I'm still pretty new at this role, but I feel like I should at least be out here observing. Do I stop him from drinking too much? Do I demand he behaves himself with threats of calling the big boss in? All four of these men play for the same team, and one is Jack's brother. How much trouble can he really get into?

I don't think I want to know the answer to that.

All of them chug down the first beer like it's a race to see who will get to the bottom first.

It's like they've done this thousands of times before even though my best guess is that these four particular men have probably never played drunk cornhole in Jack's backyard before.

Ben smashes the empty can against his forehead like some caveman once he finishes in first place, yelling "Done!" at the top of his lungs. The other three men are a little more civilized as they toss their cans on the ground and everyone reaches for another, but rowdy laughter follows Ben and his antics.

I suck in a deep breath.

I think I've got my hands full today.

"Game one, standard rules, draw for teams," Jack says, all business as he chugs a bit from his second beer. I wonder if he's hoping for a particular teammate to help assist in his victory since we all know he's going to win.

"Side bets?" Ben asks.

Jack gives him a look like it's a dumb question. "Of course. Plus a wager on each game if you're interested."

"If I'm interested." Ben scoffs at that. "Do bears shit in the woods?"

"You're an idiot," Jack says. All four of them reach into a bag to grab a beanbag. Jack and Luke both pull out red beanbags and Josh and Ben end up with black ones. I guess the teams are decided.

"What are the stakes?" Jack asks.

"Ten grand?" Ben suggests, and Jack nods.

"I'm in," Luke says, his voice full of confidence, and I can't help but wonder if the Dalton brothers are taking these other two for a ride considering they grew up together and probably played this game hundreds of times. "You?" He nods to Josh, who nods, too.

Okay, so what I'm getting here is that the winning team will walk away with twenty grand. That's a lot of money.

The guys get set up on their sides of the court then start their game. I hear Ben and Jack making their side bets—five hundred bucks you toss your bag over the board, a grand says you can't get the next three in the hole, twenty bucks to chug a beer in under ten seconds—they're all stupid, and they all make me see just how dumb men can be sometimes.

And yet...the laughter coming from the yard right now is refreshing. Seeing Jack relaxed and in his element as he has fun with his friends is a totally different dynamic than I've seen on him before. He projects this persona of always being disciplined and controlled to the entire world as he takes the field on Sundays during the season. He never sweats. He's calm under pressure—even here at home when Michelle is being awful or when JJ is crying or when he's being told a woman has been hired as his adult chaperone for nearly the next year.

He doesn't seem to ever lose his cool, but he also seems to stay pretty even-keel...which is why I like seeing him this way. These little prop bets are silly, but he's getting a kick out of them even as his speech starts to slur along with his pals and his movements start to shift from fluid and agile to a little sluggish.

The first game went to Jack and Luke, as did the second. I've lost count of the amount of beer these four have had so far, but the yard is littered with cans—a few crushed courtesy of Ben's forehead. The stakes are the same in the third game, but the score is much closer as the beer starts to affect Jack's performance. Actually, everyone seems at least a little affected by the beer except for Ben, who seems like the kind of guy who performs *better* after several drinks.

"Dude, take a video of me chugging the next beer and let's put it on my Tiktok," Ben says.

What's that old saying? Boys will be boys?

"Bad idea," I say from where I sit nearby at the patio table. "You really want all the kids who look up to you and idolize you seeing you crush a beer can on your head?"

Ben laughs like it's the funniest thing he's ever heard, and the other three follow suit. They're all idiots, but at least they let go of the Tiktok idea. For now, anyway.

The longer I sit out here, the more I think Ben Olson might need a babysitter, too. He's hot, and he's hilarious, and he's all about having a good time, but even though his cornhole play seems to have improved, his decision-making skills after a few drinks don't seem to be the best.

And Jack takes full advantage of that by luring him into prop bets he's sure to lose. There's one point when Jack is chugging a beer where I take a short video just to prove a point a little later, and he doesn't even notice when I do it.

Ben and Josh win the third game, and they take the fourth as well. The fifth game is the tiebreaker that will determine who owes who what...in addition to the running total of Ben owing Jack a little over four grand after their prop bets.

So far I haven't had to worry about much aside from the near social media blunder. They're being dumb guys, acting totally immature, and wasting a whole lot of money, but nobody's doing any harm to themselves or those around them, so my job has been fairly easy.

There's not even anything I have to report back to Calvin, and I'm grateful for that...until that tiebreaker game is interrupted halfway through when Ben says, "Anyone want to go to the club?"

Jack raises a brow. "The same club we went to the night before the trade?"

"You fucking know it, man," Ben says, and I immediately know they're talking about a strip club—both from the context and the sly smile on Ben's face. Calvin never said Jack *couldn't* go places like this, but it's still not the best idea.

"Fuck yeah," Jack says.

"I'm out," Luke says, and Josh echoes something similar. Why can't Jack be the one to echo something similar?

Ben waggles his eyebrows. "I'll drive."

My brows dip. "Oh no, you won't," I say, standing from my spot at the patio table. All eyes turn toward me in surprise that the cute little babysitter spoke up. "You've been drinking all afternoon. There's no way I'm letting you drive anywhere."

Jack shrugs. "Kia has a point. She can drive."

"I wasn't volunteering," I hiss, but they're all too far gone to catch my tone. I have to tag along either way, and at least this way I have some semblance of control and I can ensure their safety…and keep them out of headlines. "This is a bad idea," I say. "Is this really the first impression you want to leave on the Aces organization? On your new fans?"

Jack and Ben look at each other and shrug. "Fuck yeah!" they both say.

"She's not wrong," Josh says, and Luke agrees.

But Jack and Ben don't seem to care as they both dream of naked women dancing just for them. The two of them could have *any* woman they want...and I can't quite figure out what allure a strip club has other than the implicit bonds of drunkenness.

Josh and Luke call a car to drive them home—apparently they live across the street from each other.

Ben's only taller by an inch or so but Jack is the leaner of the two, so Ben hops into the front seat of my little Kia while Jack folds himself into the back, the tiebreaker game long forgotten as naked dancers take precedence.

I snap a picture of Jack in the back of my car. It's too funny *not* to, and I'm met with a glare when I check my rearview mirror to back out. I giggle. If I have to drive these two to a strip club *and accompany them* inside, at least I'm going to find little ways to enjoy it.

Ben pops open a beer in my front seat before I've even cleared the driveway.

"What are you doing?" I yell, and he's midway through chugging it when he chokes at my screeching.

Jack starts laughing in the backseat.

This is the worst idea in the history of bad ideas.

CHAPTER 16

"I can *totally* still do a cartwheel," Ben argues loudly from the front seat.

We're less than a mile away from the strip club and I've debated just turning around and going home. I'm not sure either of them would actually notice. They're still making prop bets, and the latest one has Jack insisting Ben can't do something he was able to do in his childhood.

"Prove it in the parking lot for a hundred bucks."

"You're on," Ben says. He leans in toward me. "I would've taken that bet for twenty."

I laugh. He smells like yeasty beer, and he didn't lower his voice as much as he thought he did.

"I heard that," Jack says.

Ben covers his mouth with his hand in an *oops* sort of fashion, and these two may be animals, but they're sure entertaining animals.

"What if you hurt yourself?" I ask Ben quietly. "The season's only a couple months away and a sprained wrist could really mess up your game."

"You think I can't do it?" His tone is both accusatory and mocking at the same time.

"I think you can. I just don't think you *should*."

He laughs. "Five bucks says I can."

I laugh and shake my head. "Fine. You're on." I lean in toward him and don't lower my voice, either. "I would've taken that bet for twenty."

What follows can only be described as uproarious laughter.

I pull into a space and Jack practically falls out of the backseat the second the car stops while Ben has to unwedge himself from the front. And then he proves both Jack and me wrong as he turns over in a perfect cartwheel.

I dig through my purse for a five while Jack hands him a hundred.

Ben waggles his eyebrows again. "I'd say I won't spend it all in one place, but you both know this is about to disappear into a G-string."

We head inside, and the two celebrity athletes (plus me) are lead through the main room after the hostess mentions something about a private suite for them.

I see a woman wearing the G-string Ben just mentioned doing her thing on stage as we pass through. I watch for a beat, and as much as the men in here are just objectifying women, I can't help but notice how talented this woman is. She's beautiful, and she's athletic as she moves on the pole in ways I could never dream of moving. She's confident in what she's doing where I could never dance in only a thong with people watching me.

Jack glances over at me and catches me watching, and he quirks a brow. Thank God it's dark in here, because my cheeks heat up and I'm sure I'm a bright shade of tomato red.

We're taken into the private suite, and there's no stage in here but the same music as the main room pumps loudly in here.

There's a couple couches and a pole, and a stripper walks in a minute later. She doesn't say a word as she starts dancing, and both men settle onto the couches. I'm not sure where to sit until Jack nods to the seat beside him.

I perch on the edge of the small couch, pushing myself as far away from him as I can as I think about what may have happened on this couch before I sat on it.

The distance from Jack doesn't matter. Our knees touch anyway.

I keep my eyes on the dancer even though I'm really curious to look at Jack to see his reactions to her.

Eventually she moves toward him, but he waves her off politely to let Ben take the lap dance.

Ben is basically in heaven as she grinds on his lap, and I sit awkwardly as I watch what's happening. It seems like she wants him and he wants her, and I've heard that whole thing about strippers and how part of their job is to make clients think they have a shot...but this is Ben Olson. Of course he has a shot.

He follows the rules of no touching, but she doesn't. She leans forward and licks his neck, and I feel like I'm a voyeur in someone else's bedroom. Should we even be in here?

When I glance over at Jack, though, I find his eyes on *me*.

"Enjoying the show?" he asks softly.

I lift a shoulder. "I feel like they could use some time alone."

He catches his bottom lip between his teeth, and my eyes flick there. "Would you rather watch her with me?"

I shake my head. He's drunk, and I know this, and that's where this conversation stems. He probably won't even remember it...but I will.

"Why not?" he asks softly.

Because I want you. Because I can't stop thinking about Halloween. Because I want to be the one giving you a lap dance...preferably with both of us naked so you can slide into me the way you did on a couch in a nightclub not so long ago.

A wave of heat washes over me, and I seem to mirror him as I catch my own bottom lip between my teeth. I shrug instead of giving him a real answer.

He elbows me in the arm. "Come on, Kia. It's okay to tell me."

I shake my head. I glance over at Ben, and he is now completely ignoring the *no touching* rule as his hands slide up her thighs. His mouth is hot on hers as they make out right in front of us, and her body gyrates over his like they're both completely naked.

"We should go before he gets into trouble," I say, nodding toward Ben.

Jack glances over and his eyes widen a little. "Dumbass," he mutters. He stands and moves closer to Ben before he yells into his ear, "Olson!"

Ben pushes the stripper's shoulders back just a little to break their kiss, and he looks both dazed and drunk. "What?"

"Get her number and take her home later," Jack says. He nods at the stripper, and I can't help but notice how polite he is. "You know as well as I do it's a bad idea to do this here."

Somehow Jack gets through to him, and Ben gets her number. We take off back home shortly after that, and I feel like I managed to dodge a bullet.

The car ride home is quiet, and my best guess is it's because the buzz is wearing off and now they're just tired from day drinking.

"Thanks for thinking of my rep," Ben says once I'm about to pull into Jack's driveaway. "You know I would've taken her right there."

I'm surprised he's saying this in front of me, but I shouldn't be considering he's admitting he would've just had sex in front of me without a second thought.

Drunken idiots.

"It was all Kia," Jack murmurs absently.

Ben elbows me. "Thanks, Kate," he says, using my correct name, and I press my lips together and nod once.

"My services apparently extend to any of Jack's friends on the Aces," I mutter dryly, and for some reason, that cracks up both men in the car. Maybe the buzz hasn't worn off yet.

Once Ben grabs a ride home, Jack sprawls on the couch in the family room while I make myself a plate of ham and mashed potatoes Brenda left behind. "Do you want anything?" I ask.

"I'd love a plate of whatever you're having if you don't mind," he says. "And thanks for a great day, Kia."

"Did you have fun?" I ask absently while I make a second plate.

"Yeah," he says, and I think I hear something in his voice...something forced, something that tells me he has to tell me he had fun but maybe this wasn't all he wanted out of his day. "But now I'm sober, tired, and hungry."

I finish heating our food and meet him at the kitchen table.

"Can I show you something?" I ask once we're both sitting with our plates in front of us.

He raises his brows. "You can show me *anything* you want." His voice is suggestive, and I just shake my head.

I pull out my phone and open my gallery folder then press play on the video I shot as I slide the phone toward him. He watches the video where he chugs a beer and his friend slams another can against his own forehead. He raises a brow when the video ends. "You took a video of us?"

I nod.

"Why?"

"So you could see what you looked like." I take a bite of my ham.

"Why do I need to see that?"

I shrug. "Is that how you'd want JJ to remember you?"

"There's plenty of footage of me leading teams to victories or performing community service. I fail to see how one video of an adult having some fun with his friends would paint me as some sort of villain." He pushes his plate away petulantly.

"Let me ask you a question."

He raises his brows as if to tell me to go for it.

"When you win a game, what do you remember more: the praise or the criticism?"

"The criticism," he admits. "It's always easier to believe the negative."

I nod and press my lips together. "Exactly."

He mulls that over a while as he pulls his plate back toward him and finishes eating in silence. I think I drove my point home, but that doesn't mean he's going to change his behavior anytime soon.

CHAPTER 17

"Pack an overnight bag and meet me in the truck in fifteen minutes," Jack says the next morning.

My brows dip. "Where are we going?"

"A buddy invited me onto his houseboat on Lake Mead and since Calvin thinks I'm a child, I guess you're coming with me."

My first thought is that he didn't learn anything from the video I showed him. Nothing good will come from an overnight party on a houseboat.

My second thought is *holy shit*, I've just been invited to an overnight party with celebrities on a houseboat.

And my third thought is about how much I hate fish. I know that's ridiculous, but I'll be on a boat in water. Fish live in water.

I keep my expression impassive. "May I ask which buddy?"

"No further questions." He smirks at me, and I hold in a heavy sigh as I realize he's not going to make this easy on me.

"Do you think this is a good idea?" I ask.

"Didn't I just say no questions? Get your bag packed and get down here. The truck is pulling out in..." he pauses to look at his watch. "Thirteen minutes, and I'm leaving regardless of whether you're in it."

I guess I should count myself lucky that he even told me about this trip and didn't just take off for the boat without me. I scramble up the stairs, toss the essentials into an overnight bag, throw in a swimsuit just in case since we'll be on a boat and there might be opportunities to swim, and meet him down in the kitchen in *nine* minutes. I probably forgot something, but it's one night. I'll live.

It's about forty minutes to the marina at Lake Mead, and Jack blasts Motley Crue the whole way. I recognize the music as the same classic rock my dad always plays when he's working in the garage.

It's strange to be reminded of my dad in this moment. I wonder what my parents are up to. It's a Thursday, so they're probably just finishing up their day at the diner and heading home to another cup of decaf. Predictable...the kind of existence that never really called to me.

I guess my biggest fear—even bigger than having to go back to work in a school—is ending up back home in Kansas working at the diner that was supposed to be my legacy.

He cuts the engine when he pulls into the parking lot, and the silence feels deafening after how loud the music was the whole way here.

"Motley Crue?" I tease. "I thought you were thirty-three, not fifty-seven."

His narrows his eyes at me. "Fifty-seven?"

"My dad's age," I clarify. "He's a huge fan of the Crue."

He laughs. "My dad was, too. I guess he passed down his love of football and classic rock."

"It was nice," I admit. Comforting in a way considering the sweeping changes currently in my life, not to mention the fact that I'm about to get on a houseboat with a virtual stranger and his *buddy* and who knows who else.

We get out of the car and he carries our bags toward the dock.

He hops onto one of the boats like he owns it, and then he turns toward me and holds out a hand to help me aboard.

I set my hand in his, and a dart of something travels down my spine. I think I can identify it as desire...but I'm too scared to actually label it.

I'm transported back to a couch in a nightclub at the Wynn on Halloween. His hand traveling up my leg, and his lips on mine, and his tongue moving sensually in my mouth. Our bodies rocking together as need and want plowed into each other.

That feeling is as fresh as the day I met him, but everything is different now. And that's why I can't put a label to that feeling.

His eyes meet mine, and I'm certain he feels it, too, but he doesn't say anything. Instead, I turn my eyes down to the ground. "Thanks," I mutter, dropping my hand from his like it's on fire.

"Hey!" A boisterous voice calls from another room, and then Ben appears in the doorway. "You made it!"

Ben and Jack share one of those bro hugs where they each pound the other on the back, and then Ben gives me a hug. "Hey, thanks again for saving me from making an ass of myself," he says.

I wave a hand through the air like it was no big deal. "Truth be told, you still made an ass of yourself. I just kept you out of headlines."

He laughs. "Make yourself at home here." He turns to Jack. "You're first, so pick your stateroom. Any but the master, obviously." He turns and winks at me. "That's mine. And then, we set the stakes. Oh, and all the rooms are claimed, so you two are going to have to share. Play nice...but not *too* nice." He glances at me again. "Unless you want to stay with me." This time he raises his brows, and I can tell he's kidding. At least I think he is.

My already red cheeks flush further as I realize that this means Jack and I are sharing a bedroom, which means we might also be sharing a bed.

"She'll stay with me," Jack says shortly.

Sharing a bed with Jack Dalton.

Just the thought of it causes my thighs to clench together. We didn't even share a bed the night we had sex. We were as intimate as two people could possibly be, and yet we didn't get the chance to finish the night together.

Not that we will tonight, but the thought still seems to burn brightly in my mind.

"Sure," Ben says with a knowing nod. "Anyway, get into your swim gear and let's party."

"Come on," Jack says gruffly to me, and I follow him through this houseboat toward the staterooms. He leads me through what basically looks like the first floor of a nice house. It has a kitchen with two refrigerators, dining area, couches pointed at a television, and floor to ceiling windows looking out over the water.

He walks down a hallway, and we peek into each room on the way. They all have queen beds, which would be fine if I was sharing it with my boyfriend...but I'm sharing it with Jack.

He chooses the last bedroom on the right, and he drops our bags onto the floor in there. "I didn't realize there wouldn't be a bed for my guest," he says. "But we'll figure it out. I'll just...sleep on the floor, I guess."

"It's fine, Jack. We're two adults capable of sharing a bed." I feel like maybe I jumped in too quickly, like I'm overly eager to share a bed with him. And maybe I am, but then I'm reminded why I hate him.

He grins wickedly at me. "Oh come on, Kia. We've shared more than a bed."

My cheeks turn three more shades of red.

"I'm going to get into my swim trunks. Feel free to stick around and watch."

I give him a look of horror. Is he really flirting with me when he's engaged to marry another woman? I really don't get this guy.

I grab my bag and find a bathroom where I change into my swimsuit, a red bikini with large white polka dots. I feel a little self-conscious in it, and as I rummage through my bag, I realize what I forgot: my swim coverup.

I pull my clothes back on over my swimsuit and head back to our bedroom. I knock on the door even though it's open and all I want to do is peek in, and Jack says, "Come on in, Kia. I'm decent."

It's a total lie.

Those abs are distinctly *in*decent.

He's standing in the middle of the room zipping up his duffel bag, and he's just wearing navy blue swim trunks with three white stripes on one leg. He looks hotter than fuck and I briefly debate just stripping naked and reliving our Halloween festivities, but then reality crashes back into me.

We head back to the living area, and Ben introduces us to Mickey, who will be driving the boat while we party. Mickey disappears after nodding his hellos, and then Ben turns to Jack. "So the stakes?"

Jack laughs. "Same old Ben," he says.

Ben shrugs and his mouth tips up in a half smile. "Did you expect anything less?"

Jack shakes his head with a wry smile. "What are you thinking?"

Ben thinks for a second. "I guess it shouldn't be *lady*-related since you're engaged to be married..."

"Good plan," Jack says dryly. "Poker?"

"Maybe tonight, but let's set stakes now."

Jack nods. "Alcohol-related, then?"

Ben squints a little then nods. "Yeah. I'm thinking whoever gets drunk first."

"Who judges?" Jack asks.

They both look at me. "Oh no," I say, shaking my head. "I will *not* be a party to a *who gets drunk first* bet. Not when you both know the real reason why I'm here."

Ben twists his lips. "She's got a point."

"Yeah," Jack says with a nod. "Fine."

"Let's keep it simple. Whoever chugs two beers the fastest wins five grand."

"Three beers and ten grand," Jack counters.

"You're both idiots," I say, and they both narrow their eyes at me.

"You're on," Ben agrees. "Let's head up to the upper deck where the beer is."

I sigh and lower my voice toward Jack. "How much are you planning on drinking?"

Jack shrugs. "As much as I want. I've got my babysitter here to take care of me."

Indeed.

Ben takes us up to the top floor, or what I'm going to call *the party deck*, which boasts a hot tub, a long bar complete with a bartender, stools to sit and drink, and plenty of space for a dance floor. There's also a slide from the top floor that goes down into the water below.

I'm not sure what we're here for, exactly, but some deejay shows up and starts spinning tunes loudly on the party deck, a few guys I recognize as players on the Aces arrive, and a bevy of scantily clad women ready to party show up. Seems like we're here to party.

And party we do.

Or, party *Jack* does, anyway.

Ben wins the first bet, and Jack doubles down on the stakes with a new bet—this one is who can slide down the water slide five times first. It's harder than it seems since they slide into the water and have to swim around to the stairs and climb back up to the upper deck to slide down it again.

They're both athletes, both in good shape, but Jack handily wins. More beer leads to more bets and I've lost count of who owes who what but they seem to be having fun in between Jack fending off women and Ben entertaining his guests. I'm relegated to an observer who sits in the corner. I stay out of his business so he can have fun with his friends, but still, I keep an eye on him to make sure he isn't getting himself into trouble even though he's definitely taking a turn into drunk zone.

Nothing proves that more than when a Motley Crue song starts blaring from the speakers as he's talking to Ben across the deck. He stops talking as he starts his pursuit toward me. He's dancing as he moves, and he's light on his feet with a surprising amount of rhythm. I can't help my giggle as he moves his way over toward me as the singer says I should just go away in "Don't Go Away Mad," and when he reaches out a hand to me, I take his in mine.

Would he be doing this if he wasn't eight beers deep on his friend's houseboat without his fiancée here?

Doubtful.

But he is, and as much as I want to resist because I'm torn between lust and hate for this guy, I can't. He's smiling, and he's happy, and he's drunk, and maybe this is what we needed for him to just let loose a little.

His guard is down, and even though mine should be firmly in place, it isn't. I wonder how Calvin would feel about Jack's alcohol consumption today. Would he say I'm not doing my job because I haven't attempted to stop him from drinking?

I guess it depends whether he ends up in headlines.

He's on a houseboat in the middle of Lake Mead. It's his choice to drink, and it's my job to keep him from doing something really stupid when he does. It's not my job to manage his drinking.

And so I don't. Instead, I dance with him to my favorite Motley Crue song.

"Aren't you hot in all those clothes?" he asks.

I shrug. "I'm fine."

"Have a beer with me," he says. "And look around you. Nobody's wearing clothes."

I glance around. He's right. It's either swim trunks or bikinis everywhere. I just look like the weird girl in the corner. "Fine," I mutter, and I pull off my shirt and slip out of my shorts, setting them on the chair I was just sitting in.

His eyes flick to my chest, and then they brand my body with heat as they travel down lower and back up again to meet my eyes.

He shifts on his feet a little, and then he takes a sip of beer. "That's better," he murmurs, and then he clears his throat. "We're docking tonight on a little sandbar and we're not going home until tomorrow. I promise not to get arrested. It's okay to have a little fun once in a while."

He's right. I don't need to be the boring, straight-laced, responsible one every second of every day. And so when Ben pops by a second later and presses a cold beer into my palm with a wide grin, I take it from him with a matching grin back.

When Jack's hand moves to my hip as we're dancing together, I don't bat it away. I should, but I don't.

When Ben presses another beer into my palm, it's only then I realize the first one is empty and I'm hot from dancing and being so close to Jack. I don't sip it slowly or daintily, instead giving into the fun our host is clearly trying to get me to have.

And when Jack goads me into going down the slide right after him with a promise to catch me at the bottom, I do it.

Normally I'd be terrified of the fish or potential sharks in there, but the beer has taken the edge off those fears. Or Jack has. Something has, and I'm not sure it matters what it is. Besides, I'm not sure sharks live in Lake Mead. Sharks are the real fear. Fish are just weird. I'm not *scared* of them.

As my body hits the icy cold water, I shiver...but the man who catches me warms me from the inside out. My hand accidentally brushes against his rock-hard abdomen as he helps me back toward the boat, and a shiver rises up through me.

"Get the girl another beer!" Jack yells once I'm out of the water and my feet are steady beneath me.

Some linebacker I recognize but can't name rushes over with another beer, and it's not long before I'm laughing and dancing and getting a little tipsy as I start burning up under the hot Vegas sunshine.

I don't notice the workers onboard with us, but someone lays out a buffet of Kobe burgers, beer battered onion rings, an array of salads, and an entire nacho bar.

Jack talks me into another ride down the slide to cool down before we grab a bite to eat, and the fact that he's actually hanging out with me and having fun with me feels like quite the turn in our relationship. I'd rather be friends with him than enemies. If nothing else, it'll help us both get through the next year.

I find some of the anger of our post-Halloween tryst starting to melt away even though he sort of did a number on my self-esteem that night. The beer seems to be helping to numb his annoyance of having me here, and he's almost—dare I say—being *nice* to me.

We're teetering on a dangerous cliff right now, and I'm starting to feel like I know which way I want this balance to swing. I hardly know him, but I'm having *fun* with him, and that feels good.

I just have no idea where he's at on any of it, and as I watch him and some of the other guys get involved in a friendly sparring match over their poker game later in the evening, I can't help but wonder whether he's being nice to me because he's stuck with me for the next year or if there's some other motivation at play.

CHAPTER 18

I head to bed once we're docked on our sandbar for the night. Smaller boats jetted some of the party guests back to the marina, so it's just Ben's closest friends and the women they either brought with or picked up at the party who are staying overnight.

Jack is still playing cards and I'm beat after a day in the sun drinking beer. I trust that he's not going to get arrested. He and his buddies are a little rowdy, but it's mostly just good, loud fun as they exchange chips back and forth across the table as each of them attempts to win the pot.

Jack will win. I don't need to sit there watching their game to know that. He's a champion through and through, and he never backs down until he brings home the victory. It's just who he is, and it doesn't matter if it's a friendly bet with his buddy or a poker game or a football game.

The gentle sway of the boat mixed with the alcohol and fresh air of the day lulls me quickly to sleep, but I'm pulled from my slumber when the bed shifts under Jack's weight. My heart races.

We're in the same bed. I can smell him from here, that same woodsy, masculine scent that was stamped in my memory from that night we shared, but this time mixed with the distinctive malty aroma of beer instead of gin. Even after a day in the water, he still smells like *him*.

Sharing this bed is innocent, but we're both a little drunk, and a huge part of me wants to turn in his direction and just...I don't know.

See where it leads us.

It takes everything in me *not* to do that. We have too many lines to cross, but the raw sexual magnetism between us is hard to ignore.

I only sleep in short patches after that. I try not to toss and turn, but how do I sleep when I'm overwhelmed by his scent? By *him*?

When morning comes, I wake to find us each on our own sides of the bed. Part of me thought we'd shift closer and closer to one another through the night and wake up holding each other close, and then he'd realize Michelle is all wrong for him and we'd just ride off into the sunset, maybe each holding a cup of coffee from Dunkin'.

Reality sets in. What a ridiculous dream.

I get out of bed when the need to use the bathroom becomes overwhelming, and when I return to our bedroom, he's still asleep. I watch him for a beat, and then I grab my phone and head out to the kitchen. It's deserted. I head up to the party deck to sit in one of the chairs facing the water, but I find Ben enjoying the hot tub by himself. He turns when he hears me.

"Morning," he says. I walk over closer to him instead of sitting in the chair I'd been thinking of, and I sit on the edge of the hot tub and dangle my feet in. "Sleep well?"

I shrug.

"Rough night sharing a bed with Jack?"

I chuckle. "It's completely professional between us."

He winks at me. "Sure it is. That's why he got all defensive when I offered my bed to you yesterday."

I lift a shoulder. "He's just...looking out for a friend, I guess."

"Sounds like more than friendship to this outsider," Ben says, his tone suggestive, and my curiosity gets the better of me. He *knows* Jack. Did Jack say something about me? Does he have feelings for me? "He told me you two met once before."

Oh God. I cross my fingers that the stupid cat burglar meme doesn't come up in this conversation. "Yeah," I hedge, not sure how much he knows.

"Sounds like you had a hell of a fun night before Michelle showed up."

"Yeah," I say again, not sure what, exactly, he's trying to dig out of me or what Jack told him. We *did* have a hell of a lot of fun, and he heard the story from Jack's point of view. What did he mean by a *hell of a fun night*? "But that was a long time ago. They're engaged now."

"Not happily," he mutters.

"Doesn't matter. She's wearing his ring, and that makes him off-limits."

Ben glances up at me and shakes his head. "Damn. Fine as hell *and* a moral compass. A rare combination in this business. Good for you, girl."

I blush as I laugh, and a throat clears behind us. We both turn to look and see Jack standing there looking no worse for the wear considering how much he drank last night.

"Am I interrupting something?" His voice is hoarse from sleep and he's extra sexy this morning.

Ben laughs. "We were talking about you."

My cheeks heat further.

"Oh?" Jack asks. He saunters a little closer to us and stops beside the hot tub. "What about me?"

"How drunk you got last night," Ben says. "Feeling the effects this morning?" He taps his temple to indicate a headache.

Jack shakes his head. "I'm only thirty-three, dude. I can still hold down a few beers and not wake up hungover."

I laugh. "I can't. I've got a massive headache this morning." I think that has more to do with restraining myself in a bed all night as Jack Dalton slept soundly beside me...or possibly from sleeping on a boat in a lake.

"We've got a nice breakfast spread coming out shortly," Ben says, and he leans his head back. "The coffee should be ready down in the kitchen if you need some. Help yourself to anything."

It feels like the end to our conversation, but Ben's words are stuck in my head now as I wonder what, exactly, he meant.

I follow Jack down to the kitchen and we help ourselves to coffee. The breakfast buffet is already set up, and we each grab scrambled eggs, a bunch of fruit, bacon, and pastries.

We enjoy our breakfast on the deck, and it feels like a date as we look out together over the water. I'm awkwardly silent as I think about the *hell of a fun night* we had a few months ago, and he seems to be lost in quiet thought, too.

I wish I could get into that head. I've only been here a few days, and I already know it's going to be a hard road fighting my feelings for him.

But other times...he makes it pretty damn easy.

Once we're back at the marina, we say our goodbyes to Ben and the rest of the friends we met on the boat, and we head back toward home. He blasts Motley Crue the whole way, and I can't help but wonder whether he does it so he doesn't have to talk to me.

And when we get home, it feels like all the progress we made over the last twenty-four hours is completely lost when we open the door and find Michelle sitting at the kitchen table.

"Welcome home, honey. Have fun with your little friends?" she asks snidely.

"I did," he says shortly. I notice they don't greet each other with a kiss the way you'd expect a betrothed couple to do. He glances over at me, and then he says, "Except it felt like I had a babysitter the entire time."

I raise a brow. That *is* my role here, but we haven't shared that with Michelle. She thinks I'm his assistant.

"Kind of strange to bring your assistant along," she notes, her tone hinting how she thinks something might be going on between the two of us.

"Seemed like a nice bonus," he says. He glances at me, and his expression is unreadable. "But you're right. Next time the assistant stays home."

We both know it's a lie since I need to tail him everywhere, but it still manages to punch a hole right through the fledgling friendship I'd thought we started to form.

CHAPTER 19

And so goes my first full week. Jack is a busy guy, and he's incredibly hot and cold with me. Sometimes he seems to have come to terms with having me around, though most of the time he's back in the role he thinks he needs to play. I'm frankly surprised he didn't put up a bigger fight to having me living here. Surely he wouldn't want anyone, particularly someone with a psychology background, to see the inner workings of his relationship.

My second week begins, and I counted down on the calendar last night. One week down, forty-six to go. I'm one-forty-sixth of the way to a quarter of a million bucks.

When I head down to the kitchen after my shower, it's a little before six and Jack's already in there in just a pair of mesh shorts and his Nikes.

No shirt.

A no shirt Jack is *always* a treat.

He's facing the fridge as he chugs his orange Gatorade, and the broad planes of his back are slick with sweat.

He got up early to work out, and I hate the little feeling of regret in my chest that I missed the show.

"Good morning," I say brightly. "What's on the agenda for the day?"

He ignores me and chugs the rest of his Gatorade before he slams the bottle on the counter and leaves the room.

Okay, so maybe he's not a morning person. I sit on the couch and read a few chapters in my textbook, and Brooke comes down with JJ so I chat with her for a bit.

Michelle waltzes in around ten. It seems she either ignores me or treats me like I'm *her* personal assistant, so I brace myself for what's coming today.

"I'll take a cup of coffee," she says to me, and she sashays past me and collapses onto the couch.

I'm not your fucking waitress. I don't say that, obviously, and I keep my eyes down as I move toward the kitchen so I don't get caught if I accidentally make a face at Brooke.

I think I prefer when she ignores me completely.

I grab a coffee mug from the cabinet and fill it to the top. I know she likes cream and sugar, mostly because she puts the wet coffee spoon back in the sugar bowl, but I'm feeling a little passive aggressive this morning. I hand the black coffee to her and settle back on the couch, opening my textbook as I pretend to read.

She sighs heavily and mutters something about if you want something done right, you need to just do it yourself.

Amen, girlfriend. A-freaking-men.

"I'm off to work," she says to Brooke. She plants a kiss on JJ's head but doesn't otherwise engage with him, and then she dumps her full cup of coffee into the sink and walks out of the room.

I hate her a little more every day, and the house is much brighter after she leaves for work.

When lunchtime rolls around and I still haven't seen Jack, I decide to check the little app on my phone just to make sure he didn't take off. He's still in the house—or at least his phone is.

After a quiet lunch by myself, I wander around the house a bit until I end up near Jack's office. I hear his voice on the phone through the closed door.

"I can't keep doing this. It's all so fucked. There *has* to be another way."

What can't he keep doing? I didn't mean to overhear him, but I did.

I'm sure he wouldn't want me to listen in on his conversation, so instead of eavesdropping, I simply knock on the door.

"I'll call you later," I hear him say into the phone, and then he yells, "What?"

I open the door and peek my head in. "Everything okay?" I ask.

"No." He presses his lips together, and even though he didn't invite me in, I walk in anyway and slide into the chair across from him.

"Care to talk about it?" I ask.

"No," he repeats. He's cranky today.

"You know I'm going to be around for nearly the next year, right?" I press. "You can talk to me."

"Look, Kia. You can't just shrink me like one of your little patients."

I raise a brow. "For starters, my name is Kate, not Kia. And I'm not here to shrink you. Your boss believed you would benefit from a different sort of coach than you typically interact with on the field, and that's why I'm here."

He raises a brow and holds out his hands. "All right. Then coach me."

"Well, what behaviors do we need to change?" I ask.

He shrugs. "None. I guess that means we're done here."

I laugh. "I don't think we are. Calvin is worried about your ability to be a team player."

"Pfft," he scoffs. "Please. I know how to be a team player."

"Do you?" I ask. "Because it seems you wanted out of Denver because your coach wouldn't let you have total control of your offense."

"Because I know how to run my offense," he protests.

"Better than the man being paid to make those calls?" I ask. Thank God I did my research here. "Look, Jack, sometimes you need to set your ego aside and let other people do their jobs."

"Like you?" he asks. He leans back in his chair and crosses one leg casually over the other at the knee.

I shrug. "I mean you *could* make it a little easier on me."

"Where would the fun in that be?" he asks, and just the way he looks at me tells me how freaking big that...*ego* of his is.

I ignore his words. "Your actions aren't just about you. They reflect everywhere." I'm trying to get him to see how his own ego is paralyzing him.

"I'm aware of who my actions affect. And for the record, I don't give a fuck about anything except my son and football."

"What about Michelle?"

My question is met with a beat of silence, and it's a clear confirmation about the reasons behind his current actions. He further reinforces it by adding, "I said what I said."

"Luke mentioned your father's will at dinner. What's in it?"

"I don't have to tell you anything," he says petulantly.

"You're right. You don't." I nod and press my lips together, and then I decide to just go for it. "But we have a bit of a history together, and you were quite an asshole to me more than once, and maybe letting me in will make the next forty-six weeks a little more bearable for us both."

"Forty-six weeks?" he repeats. "You counted them?"

I lean back in my chair casually, too. "You know, I was a nanny for a couple years, and every time Kennedy, the little girl

I took care of, was excited about something coming up—like a vacation, or a field trip, or whatever—we'd make one of those little paper chains to count down until that special day arrived." I smile at the memory, and then I meet his gaze to see if he decoded my underlying meaning.

"And you're excited for what happens in forty-six weeks?" he guesses.

"Bingo!" I shoot him a sweet smile.

He sighs. "Why are you doing this, then?" he asks.

"Oh, no, Mr. Dalton. You're not turning the tables on me. We're here to talk about you." I point toward his chest.

"Maybe if *you* let *me* in a little, I'll be more comfortable doing the same."

I snort-laugh in a very unladylike way. "Right. And I'll be on the next Space X mission to Mars."

He narrows his eyes at me. "Elon wouldn't put you in space."

I raise a brow. "And why not?"

He lets a little smile slip through. "Cats in space?" He shakes his head. "I think he's more of a dog guy."

I purse my lips to hide my smile. "You're doing it again."

"What?" he asks, his face the picture of innocence.

"Turning the tables on me." I cross my arms over my chest as I make a snap decision. "You tell me the truth about your relationship with Michelle and I'll tell you why I'm really here."

He stares me down for a beat. His eyes are stormy and intense, but it's not a product of this conversation. They're always like that. It's as if he's trying to decide how much he can trust me, and I feel like he's leaning toward giving me a little tidbit simply so he can have a little tidbit about me.

That's the thing about athletes. They study their opponents, and sometimes they have to give a little to learn where weaknesses might lie so they can pounce later.

"She dated my brother, fucked me for revenge when they broke up, got pregnant, said it was his, turned out to be mine, had the baby, and I proposed." He shrugs. "Now you go."

"I don't think so, buddy," I say as I shake my head. I realize too late I used to call Miles *buddy* all the time. It's a term of endearment that just slipped out and stuck, but I don't want to give Jack a term of endearment. Especially not when he calls me *Kia* all the damn time...and also because of that whole thing about making it harder to let things go once you've named them. "You told me things I already know, not the truth about your relationship. Why did you propose?"

He stills after slightly jutting out his chin, a telltale sign he's about to tell a lie. "Because we share a child."

"Why else?" I press.

He raises a brow. "Because it felt like the right thing to do."

"What are you getting out of it?"

He's silent, but his chin is still raised a bit in defense.

I try a different tack. "What is *she* getting out of it?"

He blows out a breath and uncrosses his leg. He scoots forward in his chair and folds his arms on his desk in front of him, and then he glances up at me before his eyes fall back down onto his hands.

So there *is* something. There's some reason a marriage is mutually beneficial to them. I just don't know what it is yet.

But I *will* get to the bottom of it.

CHAPTER 20

"I need to go to the hospital," Jack declares when he walks into the kitchen freshly showered the next morning. He smells as divine as usual as he passes by where I sit at the table, and I breathe the air in subconsciously as I take that scent into my lungs before I realize what I'm doing.

It's early—a little after seven—and I'm ready to go since I've been getting up at the crack of dawn just in case he needs to go somewhere in the morning and doesn't have time to wait for me to get ready.

Well, that added on top of the fact that I don't really want him to see what I look like just having freshly rolled out of bed. I've only been here a week. I'm not quite ready for that yet.

My brows dip as worry fills me—worry for a situation I know nothing about other than Jack announcing the next location on his very busy agenda. "Is everything okay?"

He nods, and when he turns to look at me, he has a soft smile on his face. "Ellie had the baby."

"How exciting," I gush. "Congratulations, Uncle Jack."

His soft smile lifts a little as he shakes his head. "I thought it'd be Kaylee's kids calling me that first, not Luke's." He pauses, and then he adds, "Though I didn't think I'd be called *Daddy* before either of those events. Except, you know, in bed."

He waggles his eyebrows, and I can't help my laugh.

"Are you ready to go?" he asks, and I nod. "Get in the truck." His tone is gruff, but there's a bit of teasing in it, too.

He blasts Motley Crue the whole way there, and he seems to have a particular affinity for their *Dr. Feelgood* album, which is cool since my dad does, too. We pull into a parking space, and he grabs a ballcap from the backseat. He pulls it down low over his eyes, and we head into the hospital.

"Are you sure it's okay I'm here?" I ask.

Jack shrugs. "I guess we're a package deal for the short term." He still sounds annoyed by that, but I feel like I sense a little less irritation than last week. I count it as progress.

He texts Luke to let him know we're here then stops at the gift shop for the biggest blue balloon arrangement in the place plus a flower arrangement for Ellie. Luke greets us in the lobby and laughs at the over-the-top balloons.

"Congratulations, man," Jack says to his brother, and the two meet in the middle for a hug as Jack claps him on the back. "How's it feel?"

Luke shakes his head and lets out a breath. "Incredible. Terrifying. Amazing. Exhausting." He lets off a little chuckle. "He was born at three in the morning and I haven't slept more than an hour at a time in over forty-eight hours now."

I hug him, too, and offer my own congratulations. And holy shit, I'm hugging Luke Dalton. What even is this life?

Jack laughs during our quick hug. "Get used to it, but it'll pass. How's he doing? And Ellie?"

"Both are perfect," Luke says. His lips tip softly at the corners. "Beyond perfect. Come meet him." He turns to lead us to Ellie's room.

"I'll just wait here," I say, not wanting to interrupt this sweet family moment. It's not like Jack is going to get arrested here in the hospital.

Jack turns around with his brows knit together. "Nonsense," he says.

He flicks his neck in one of those *come on* motions just as Luke says, "Come on."

I guess I'm part of this, which feels strange since it should be Jack's fiancée here...though I can't think of a single person who will be in that room who'd actually *want* her there.

I follow him through the halls to the maternity ward, and he brings us straight to their room where Ellie is lying on the bed and the baby is in a bassinet beside her. Jack leans down to hug his sister-in-law. "How're you feeling?" he asks.

She smiles, and she looks exhausted but beyond elated. "Tired and a little sore, but I've never been happier." Her eyes land on her husband, and the emotion that passes between the two of them is so strong that I can feel it as a total outsider.

"Congratulations," I say softly, my eyes feeling a little misty as I glance over at the sweet baby boy sleeping beside his mother. "What's his name?"

"Nolan Timothy Dalton," Ellie says.

Jack turns to Luke with surprise. "Timothy?"

Luke presses his lips together. "Ellie let me pick the middle name."

"What an amazing tribute to Dad," Jack says, and I gather Timothy was his name. "He would've been so proud of you."

Luke shrugs with modesty, but it's clear there's an underlying respect, appreciation, and love between the brothers. When I was researching Jack's history, though, I got the impression it wasn't always that way.

It is now. That's all that matters.

"I don't want to wake him, but I had to stop by to see him and congratulate you both," Jack says softly. He looks between Luke and Ellie. "You two are going to be the most amazing parents. Nolan is a lucky boy."

"He's also lucky he has a cousin four months older than him whose father will surely show both boys all the things we'll have to undo," Ellie jokes.

Jack laughs and messes up his brother's hair affectionately, and Luke pushes him away. For a second, it's like they're little boys messing with one another, and it's sort of totally adorable.

We say our goodbyes and take off without ever having gotten to hold the baby, but I'd still venture to say that this trip to the hospital was a turning point.

Jack is becoming more and more human every day to me, and that can only spell trouble where my heart is concerned.

CHAPTER 21

It's early afternoon when I realize I need to get a move on figuring out my plans for Shannon's bachelorette party. I head toward Jack's office, where I hear voices inside.

I knock on the door.

"Yeah?" Jack yells.

I open it and find Michelle sitting in the chair across from him. She's wiping under her eyes, and Jack looks frustrated.

"Oh, I'm so sorry. I can come back later," I say, and I turn to leave when I hear his voice.

"It's fine," he says. "We're done here."

"No we aren't," Michelle protests.

"Uh, yeah, Michelle. We are. I have work to do."

"Right," she says. "For your little company." She sniffles, and then she stands, and it's like her entire demeanor completely shifts. Gone are the tears, replaced now with...I don't even know what this is. She points a finger at him. "You *better* be there."

He scoffs. "Or what?"

"Or I'll get Daddy involved."

He rolls his eyes. "Do what you have to do. Kia and I have some business to discuss, so close your door on the way out."

It's his not-so-gentle way of giving her the boot, and she huffs past me on her way out without so much as a glance in my direction.

"What was that about?" I ask once the door slams shut behind her.

He raises his brows and shakes his head as he keeps his eyes down on some paperwork in front of him. "Yet another emotional outburst."

"Is everything okay?"

He shrugs. "Sure." He pauses and looks up at me, and his expression is schooled as he gives me a smile. It's not genuine, though. It doesn't reach his eyes, and it looks like the one I've seen him use with the media after losing a game. "Everything's great. Can't wait to marry a master manipulator who brings her father into every argument we have." He says the last part under his breath, but it's still loud enough for me to catch.

I can't tell if he's just stewing over whatever fight he just had with her or if this is his way of letting me in, but I can't let this chance get away from me. "Are you in love with her?"

I'm met with silence.

I wait for him to answer, and when I've counted to twenty and he still hasn't, I press a little harder. "Or are you marrying her because you feel like you don't have a choice?"

"I *don't* have a choice," he finally admits.

"There's always a choice, Jack," I say quietly. I tuck my bangs behind my ear. I'm trying to talk him out of doing the very thing Calvin is paying me to get him to do. I'm putting my own job security at risk.

But I need him to know he has an out. My job is to help him make better decisions, right?

Calvin wants me to keep him in check so Jack will marry his daughter and score touchdowns for his team. He's not *really* paying me to get inside Jack's head.

It *is* quite the love story, though, isn't it? Quarterback marries the owner's daughter. It's the stuff of movies, except in the movie, the couple is actually in love.

"Not for me," he grits out. "Not when my life has been planned for me."

My brows dip. "What do you mean?"

He shakes his head. "First it was my own father, and now it's her father."

"Tell me more about your father," I say.

His gaze moves to the window. "He died in October."

"You mentioned that before," I say softly. "And I'm so sorry. May I ask what happened?"

"Aneurism. He was here one minute, gone the next." He snaps his fingers.

"That's terrible. Is that why your mom moved out here?"

"Yeah." He nods.

"Is that when your behavior started to change?" I ask, and his eyes dart back to mine in surprise. I tilt my head as I level my gaze at him. "Why does that question surprise you?"

He shrugs. "It's rare to find someone willing to dig a little deeper. Once you mention a parent's death, everyone wants to express their condolences and then move onto something else."

I shrug. "Not me."

He stares at me a long beat, and I can't help but try to figure out what he's thinking. I hope he knows I actually care about him. This isn't about me being paid to dig a little deeper, as he said. It's about truly coaching him to make the best choices for himself. "So is that when?" I ask again, trying to get to the bottom of when he started to transition from a dedicated and serious football player into a partying playboy.

"Not really, but it didn't help." He leaves it at that.

"Your brother mentioned the will at dinner when he was asking about Michelle. How are the two related?"

He's frustratingly silent.

"Come on, Jack. Give me something to work with," I beg.

"Look, Kia," he says, rubbing his eyes with the heels of his palms. "I've got a lot of work to do." It's his easy way of dismissing me, but I don't budge from my chair. "You can go now."

I clear my throat. "What kind of work does a football player do in the off season?"

"Real estate," he says.

"Investing?" I ask.

He nods. "Among other responsibilities, yes. I own a real estate development company, so most of the year I delegate. But when I'm not playing, I sit in with the team I've built in my own company."

"So you *have* learned to let some control go," I say.

He chuckles. "To some degree, I guess. I try to put the right people in the right places, but there's still a lot I need to do."

I clear my throat and twist my hands in my lap, determined to get out my question before I leave this office. "I, um, I know you're a busy guy, and since you didn't give me access to your calendar..."

"Yes?" he asks, drawing out the word as he can see that I'm about to make a request.

"What are your plans Saturday night?" I blurt.

"I'm going out with my boys," he says.

My chest tightens in disappointment. "Oh," I say, nodding. "Okay. I'll have to check with Calvin to see if someone can sit in for me then. Can't have you running all over town unsupervised."

"Why?" he asks. "Where will you be?"

"My best friend is getting married next weekend and this weekend is her bachelorette party. I'm a bridesmaid and I completely forgot to ask for the night off when Calvin hired me," I admit.

"Is your friend a football fan?" he asks with a smirk.

I blow out a breath and decide to go for broke. "My friend is the one who pushed me in front of you on Halloween."

His jaw slackens a little at that, and I can't help a little smirk of my own. "She pushed you in front of me?"

I shrug. No sense in lying about it now. "She thought it would give me a shot with you."

He lifts a brow, clearly a little impressed. "She wasn't wrong."

We both laugh, though the stark reminder of our night together sends another pulse between my legs.

"What about Kitty Kate?" he asks out of the blue.

My brows draw together in confusion.

"You know, like Kitty Cat? But with Kate instead." He tilts his head and twists his lips. "I could go with Kitty Kia."

"Kia is fine." My eyes widen as I realize what I just said. "Shit! I mean Kate! My name is *Kate*!"

He grins at how totally flustered I am, and my cheeks redden with horror.

"Sure it is, Kia." He nods and gives me a wink, and I just sink back into my chair, completely mortified.

CHAPTER 22

Later in the afternoon, I slide into the chair across from Jack in his office to get the final word on this weekend when Michelle strides into the room like she owns it. I guess technically it's her dad's house, so in that sort of way, she does own it.

"What are you doing?" she demands.

She plops into the empty chair beside me, but she doesn't actually acknowledge my presence. She doesn't seem to notice that we might've been in the middle of a conversation.

"Working," Jack says pointedly.

"Oh, on your cute little company?" she asks, her tone dripping with something. Sarcasm, maybe?

"It's neither cute nor little," Jack says. "Do you need something?"

"They called me back out to Los Angeles," she says. "I leave Thursday. I need to talk wedding stuff with you in my office before I go."

I pick apart her words, starting at the top.

Who is *they*?

Why is she going to Los Angeles?

None of it is any of my concern, I suppose, but she has piqued my curiosity.

"Fine," Jack says, and then he turns to me. "Hey, personal assistant. Can you find time in my calendar for a wedding planning meeting with my bride to be?" His tone drips with something, too. I'm not sure whether it's sarcasm or disgust, though.

My eyes widen. He *knows* he didn't give me access to his calendar, and now he's playing some game. I think I might be the pawn in it. I'm a little confused.

"Of course, Mr. Dalton," I say sweetly. I open my own calendar to make this act look legit. "Looks like Thursday at noon is open."

Michelle blows out a breath and looks at me like I'm stupid. "I *leave* Thursday. I need before then."

"Oh, right," I say, and I catch Jack's eye. His are full of merriment, and I look down at my calendar again so I don't accidentally start to giggle. "That's my bad. Hm." I review my calendar that's pretty much wide open, and she stares daggers at me as she waits.

"Right now looks open." I lock eyes with Jack, and I shrug and shoot him a sweet smile.

His gaze hardens, and I stifle a laugh.

"Now's not good," he says. "I have a contract I need to review."

"Come on, Jack," she whines.

"Give me an hour," he finally concedes, but the hesitation in his voice is loud and clear.

"Okay. I'll just wait here, then." She pauses a beat, and then she asks, "What contract are you reviewing?"

"I don't have time to chat right now, dear," Jack says, his voice using that same condescending tone he hits me with sometimes.

"Just trying to show some interest in my husband's little company," she mutters.

"Will you *please* stop calling it little?" Jack booms, and her brows crinkle.

"Oh, I'm sorry. I just always think of companies with fewer than twenty employees as *little*." She gives him a fake smile, and my fingers flex on my lap as a bit of defensiveness creeps over me. I'm not even sure why. I have nothing to defend, but seeing the way she treats him is pressing on a nerve I didn't realize I had.

"We have twenty exactly now," he says, nodding at me, "so I guess we're not so *little* anymore."

Wait a minute. *I* am his newest employee?

"Didn't Daddy hire her?" she asks, giving him a look like he's dumb.

He ignores her as his eyes move back to his computer screen. "And we have several multi-million-dollar deals going at all times, not that I need to defend my company to you."

"That's wonderful," she says, and her tone clearly conveys that it's not and she doesn't give a rat's ass. "Let me know when the dollars start pouring in, 'k?"

Jack sighs. "Look, Michelle. The more you interrupt me from my work now, the less time we'll have to talk later."

She holds up both hands innocently. "Okay, okay," she says. She pulls her phone out from her cleavage and starts tapping around on it.

Loudly. And obnoxiously.

I think she's texting, but I'm trying not to be nosy. It's just that her nails keep tapping the screen and it's like...well, it's like nails on a chalkboard, but instead it's a phone screen. Jack glances up pointedly at her hands, but she's totally oblivious to just how irritating she is.

"I can meet you in your office when I'm ready," Jack says.

"Oh, no, I'm fine waiting in here."

"Michelle," he says, his voice firm. "Go." He nods toward the door, and her gaze lifts to him.

"*She* gets to stay," she argues, finally acknowledging that there is another person in the room.

"*She* is my assistant," he says. "She has work to do. I will meet you in your office in an hour."

She pins him with a glare but eventually does get up to do what she's told. She stalks out of the room and slams the door behind her.

Sounds like that'll be a real fun meeting in an hour. I'm frankly shocked he didn't make me leave, too.

I'm not quite sure what I'm supposed to do now. Do I leave? Our conversation seems to be over, and his mood seems to have soured since his fiancée stopped by.

But I sort of just want to sit here a few minutes and let her clear out. I don't want to run into her in the kitchen because I don't really care for her. And it's not just because she's engaged to Jack and I wouldn't care for *anyone* cast in that role.

It's more because she's a terrible person.

"Do, uh...do you really have something for me to do?" I finally ask.

He closes his eyes for a beat, and then he finally looks up at me. The look there in his eyes clearly says *get the fuck out* without the words leaving his mouth. He needs to review his contract, and he needs to concentrate, and these constant interruptions are only setting him back.

Unlike his future bride, I can take a hint.

I get up and walk out without another word. Michelle's office is around the corner from Jack's and on the way toward the kitchen, and I hear two voices talking quietly as I approach.

"I heard back," one woman's voice says, and I don't recognize it.

"And?" Michelle asks.

"They said yes!"

I shouldn't eavesdrop, but their little squeals make me stop in my tracks.

"They don't care that Tristan's out?" Michelle asks.

"They said it's even better. We'll have a totally different angle they weren't even expecting and it'll give me a storyline with the recovery and all that."

"I thought he filed for divorce, though," Michelle says.

"Oh, he did. But I can be *very* convincing when I want to be."

Both women laugh, and there's an edge of maliciousness in their conversation that make me feel very uncomfortable.

I don't know who this woman is, but she seems an awful lot like Michelle. And having two of them around most definitely won't help Jack when it comes to *my* purpose here, which is helping him make better decisions.

Because unless he decides to leave Michelle, I just don't see how I can coach him to do the right thing without losing my job.

CHAPTER 23

Jack saunters down into the kitchen in Aces workout gear the next morning. "We're heading to the Complex today," he says. "We leave in ten minutes."

"What's the *Complex*?" I ask.

"The practice facility." He says it like this is something I should know.

"Okay," I say, even though what I *really* want to say is something about how it would've been nice to know that yesterday if I had some freaking access to his damn calendar.

I climb into his truck and hold on for dear life as he weaves in and out of traffic. "I need to go to Los Angeles tomorrow. I emailed you the details just before we left so you can book your travel while you wait around for me today."

"What for?" I ask, wondering whether this has something to do with Michelle.

"Aren't you full of questions?" he murmurs.

I chuckle. "Just wondering what's on tap."

"I'll be fucking around with some friends and we'll probably hit the strip clubs. I'll do what I can to get arrested, and for sure I'll make headlines probably with whatever stripper is the hottest. And since Los Angeles is, well, the city of angels, and I've never met an angel I didn't want to fu—"

"All right, all right," I say, holding up a hand as I cut him off. At least I'm starting to get a little bit of a read on him. Sometimes. "What are you *really* going to do?"

He laughs. "I need to meet with my agent and I'm scheduled to film an endorsement spot. Does all that meet with your approval?"

I purse my lips and cross my arms over my chest. "It's fine."

We ride in silence, and I don't get why sometimes he's such a dick and other times he's almost semi-nice to me. His moods swing wildly and it's like I'm on a roller coaster I can't seem to get off.

"What are you doing at the Complex today?" I ask as I try to make conversation.

"Meeting some of the coaches and a few of the guys on the offensive line for a casual workout. It's just for whoever's in town and free to swing by."

"And you're proving you're a team player by showing up?"

"Bingo," he says with a smile. "See? My ego isn't *that* big."

I snort, and he narrows his eyes in my direction.

"I've been in the business long enough to realize the importance of building a team from the word *go*, and they didn't bring me here to sit on a bench even though Calvin keeps making empty threats." He floors it as a light turns yellow rather than stopping. "They brought me here to fucking win, and the sooner I get to know the men on my line, the sooner we can start working to earn our Ws."

"Will your brother be here today?"

He lifts a shoulder. "Probably not. He's not doing full workouts yet with his knee still in recovery."

"Do you know any of the other guys you'll be playing with?" I ask.

"A few. Some through my brother, some because I've played against them. You get to know some guys, get to be friendly with others."

"Even with the enemy?" My tone is light.

His answer is not. "Better to know your enemy, right?" I can't help but think we're no longer talking about football.

I'm just not sure whether he means me, Michelle, or somebody else entirely.

We arrive at the Complex, and he heads toward a locker room. He deposits me in a room that looks like a classroom on the way. It's a small room with two rows of tables set up five tables deep each. Each table has two chairs behind it, and they all face forward to a single desk at the front of the room with a huge screen behind it. "I have a meeting in the room across the hall from here before the workout. You can wait in here until we're done with the meeting, and then we're heading to the weight room on the opposite side of the building. There's a community room over there where families can watch workouts, so you can go there."

"Aw, you think of me as family?" I ask.

He chuckles. "You're basically like my mother."

I wrinkle my nose. "Please don't ever say that again."

This time the chuckle turns into a full-on laugh.

"How long will you be?" I ask.

He shrugs. "Don't know. It's my first meeting as an Aces teammate." He leaves at those words and heads across the hall, and I'm left to my own devices.

I find the email he sent me with his flights. He gave me the contact information to book the open first-class tickets next to him, so I call the airline and with the snap of a finger, my flights are booked.

I can't say I'm not a little excited at the chance to go to Los Angeles...even though it's for work.

I also can't say I'm not totally terrified to travel alone with Jack Dalton. Not because of the job. So far he's made that pretty easy.

But because I'm a little worried about the threat he poses to my heart. I hated him with an icy passion at first, but that hate has thawed into something else. Fire tends to do that to ice.

His meeting lasts about a half hour, and I hear jubilation and excitement coming from the room across the hall throughout those thirty minutes since they left the door open. I can't really make out the specifics, but I can both hear and feel the excitement in the air.

Jack peeks his head into my room. "Come on," he says, and I jump up to join him—mostly because I'm certain I'll get lost in these hallways without an escort.

"This is my assistant, Kia," he says by way of introduction, and my eyes widen as I'm suddenly surrounded by four members of the Vegas Aces. "And this is Jaxon Bryant, Cory Marshall, Andre Irvin, and you know Josh Nolan."

"Oh my God," I murmur, and my brain completely misses that Jack just called me Kia. I know who every single one of these men is, and despite the fact that I've been working with Jack over the last couple weeks and I've met his brother and Josh, it's still a little surreal to be standing in these hallways like this is all normal to just be introduced to some of the greatest running backs and receivers to ever take the field. "I can't believe I'm standing here with all of you."

"She's not a crazy fan," Jack says.

"Damn," Cory says, and he offers me a teasing grin. "She had some good potential until you said that."

An older man appears from the doorway of the classroom where they just held their meeting, and he looks familiar, like I've seen him standing on the sidelines on Sundays as I watched the Aces games on television. "The others should already be in the weight room," he says, and he moves to the front of the pack and starts his trek in that direction. The men all turn to follow him with Jack up in front, and I head up the back of the pack, still a little shaken that I'm in the presence of all this greatness.

I'm in a daze as we approach the weight room, and Jack hangs back. He points to a room with a wall of windows that overlooks the weight room. "You can wait in there," he says. The room is empty right now, but it looks like the kind of place where team families with children can hang out or where maybe groups of fans could pay or win their way in to watch workouts. It's outfitted with couches and televisions and tables with chairs, and the back half of the room is fully dedicated to entertainment for kids.

A brief flash of a future toddler JJ flashes through my mind as I settle in by myself. I haven't spent a ton of time around him since he's at daycare most days and Brooke keeps him occupied in the evenings, but I can imagine driving him over to watch his daddy run through his workouts.

I glance at Jack on the other side of the glass. His eyes meet mine, and that same heat that always passes between us is there.

Someone must call his name, because he breaks our gaze and turns toward one of the other guys he's working out with.

And then reality plows into me.

My job here only lasts through February. I probably won't get the chance to see a toddler JJ as he watches daddy through the glass. I won't get to hear his first words.

He's not mine to care for even if I'm starting to fall for him.

And it's that final thought that drives a wedge of confusion right through my heart.

I don't know if I'm referring to JJ...or to his daddy.

Either way, I think I'm screwed. It's time to change the direction of this ship before things get really complicated.

CHAPTER 24

We take a car provided by the credit card company Jack will be filming a commercial for to the airport. In fact, the company is paying for basically everything on this trip.

It makes me realize how big a deal Jack Dalton actually is.

"Do you like traveling?" I ask on our way toward the airport.

"Love it," he says. "But the majority of my travel is work-related, so I don't get to really enjoy the cities I'm in. It's always a circus anyway when I try to get out."

"That night we went to dinner with your family—that wasn't a circus," I point out.

He shakes his head. "No, you're right. Because we rented out the back-half of the place and positioned ourselves so nobody would spot us."

I hadn't realized all that.

"That's the kind of life I live," he continues, "and unless I'm being paid to be seen somewhere, it's easier to just stay home."

"But you don't."

He shakes his head. "Nah. Where's the fun in that?"

"Will you have time for fun this trip? A chance to enjoy the city?"

He lifts a shoulder and stares out the window. "The agenda is tight. As my assistant, you should probably know my schedule is all booked up."

"Where are we at on that whole shared calendar thing?" I ask.

He laughs. "Same place we've always been." He takes a screenshot of something on his phone and texts it to me. "That's our agenda for the next two days."

I read it over. As soon as we land, we'll be ushered to a studio to practice filming the commercial. Then we'll be taken to dinner, where we will dine with credit card executives. We'll be released to our hotel, and in the morning we'll shoot the commercial. We're scheduled to be done by three, and our flight back to Vegas is at five.

I see what he means about not having the chance to enjoy the city he's in while he's there.

"What about you?" he asks. "Do you like to travel?"

I nod. "Yeah. I haven't done a ton of it. My parents are both hard workers and had small windows of days off, so our trips were usually drivable and fairly local. Vegas was the furthest west I'd been when I moved here for college."

His gaze is fixed down on his hands. "My family took vacations when I was younger. Then I went off to college and was drafted and it got harder and harder. My little sister started a tradition where we meet somewhere for a week every summer. It was the only week out of the year my entire family got to be together for more than a day or two at a time."

"That sounds fun," I say. "Where did you go last year?"

"Hawaii," he says. "Luke and Ellie got married while we were all there. I was an asshole." He scrubs a hand along his jaw and winces a little, and I get the impression there's a level of regret involved in that. Admitting it is the first step toward healing, though.

"But you're all on good terms now," I point out.

He nods. "Yeah. We are. It was a rough road getting back there, and I certainly didn't make it any easier. But you can't live life with regrets." His eyes are out the window again. "I guess you just..." He shrugs. "Move forward."

We're dropped at a private entrance I didn't know existed at this airport, ending that conversation, but I feel like he opened up just a little. I can only hope he continues to do so as we spend time together over the next two days.

We land in Los Angeles, just as the agenda he sent me said, and we're ushered off to a skyscraper downtown. Once we're in the lobby, Jack strolls over toward a man grinning at him as he walks toward us. They meet in the middle for a handshake-turned-slap-on-the-back-hug.

"Tom, this is Kate," Jack says, introducing the two of us. "Kate, this is my agent, Tom."

"Tom Levinson," he says, reaching out a hand to shake mine. His eyes are intense—dark but still friendly, and he looks like the kind of guy who can be a shark in the boardroom as he cuts business deals, but he can be a trustworthy and loyal friend, too. He's quite attractive, and it's those intense eyes that sort of just draw me in. "A pleasure to meet you." He glances at Jack. "She's the babysitter?"

"The assistant," Jack says thickly, but there's still merriment in his eyes at his agent's teasing.

"They're waiting for us upstairs," Tom says, and we follow him toward a bank of elevators.

Once we're upstairs, we're ushered back to a conference room. Introductions are made, and we all sit around the table a few minutes while the executives in the room explain what Jack will do.

After about an hour, Tom and I are led to the room next door. Our conference room has a window that looks over the room Jack is in. It's one of those one way mirror windows, and I keep my eyes trained on Jack as I stand in front of it.

Tom comes up to my side and looks at Jack with me.

"He's different with you, you know."

My eyes don't leave Jack as I ask, "How?"

"I've known him a lot of years. I've been with him since the beginning. I've seen him through Savannah, through some actresses, a stripper or two, a singer, a few models, escorts, all the other random girls he picked up at bars, women he was with on nightclub couches..." He clears his throat meaningfully. Okay, I get it. He knows Jack and I were once together. "He wasn't like this with any of them. Apart from Savannah and Michelle, he didn't keep any of them around more than a couple nights. He didn't *nickname* any of them, and yet you're Kia." He shakes his head as he stares at Jack. "His whole demeanor is different. He seems more...relaxed. At first I figured it was because Michelle wasn't here, but now I'm wondering if it's because you *are* here."

I glance over at Tom, but I don't know what to say.

His eyes meet mine when he turns toward me, and then he looks at Jack again. "He doesn't love Michelle." His tone is flat.

"I know."

"So what does that mean for you?" he asks.

My eyes are trained on Jack again. I don't know how much to give up to this guy. I don't know what will get back to Jack. And so I settle on the truth as I see it. "It means Jack is engaged to another woman. Until that stops being true, it means I'm his behavior coach."

"Right." Tom nods, and that's the end of that conversation.

I wish I had the nerve to ask more questions of one of the few people who seems to know Jack well, but I don't.

* * *

I'm a little tipsy.

I'm not *drunk*, but the dinner included wine with each course and my tolerance is shot since my job taking care of two kids for the last two years didn't allow much time for drinks.

One of the executives handed Jack a key to a hotel room downtown somewhere, and once the car deposits us into the lobby of said hotel, we take the elevator up to the room.

It's just the two of us, and it's quiet in here.

Is it just me, or is there an underlying sexual tension burning between us?

It's just me. Definitely. Or the wine. At least I think it is until I meet his eye in the reflection of the elevator door and a certain heat passes between the two of us.

Maybe it's not just me.

He opens the door to our suite, and there's a huge room with a couch and a big table with six chairs. It must be some sort of executive suite. We walk through the room toward a door to the bedroom, and sure enough...there's just one bed. I spot both our suitcases on racks inside the closet. How'd they get here before us?

"I'll sleep on the couch," I offer.

His eyes meet mine. "Nonsense. It's a king. We can just..." He shrugs. "Sleep on our own sides."

"Whatever," I mutter, mostly because I'm freaking tired after traveling and then all the wine.

I walk over to my suitcase and grab the items I need to get ready for bed, and then I disappear into the bathroom for a few minutes. The wine hasn't really let up yet, and part of me wants to walk out of the bathroom completely naked and seduce Mr. Jack Dalton.

I don't, obviously, but wine makes me horny. Or Jack does. And the combination of the two should be illegal.

I choose my side of the bed while he uses the restroom next. I sit on top of the covers and pull up the book I was reading on the Kindle app on my phone.

He emerges from the restroom wearing just a pair of mesh shorts a minute later, and I squeeze my legs together to try to help keep the ache suddenly between them in check.

It doesn't help.

I keep my eyes focused down on my phone. I have to.

It's the hardest thing I've ever had to do.

"You're on my side," he says.

"Should've gone first, then," I retort, and he chuckles as he climbs in beside me.

The king size bed seemed big when I was standing on the floor looking at it, but when Jack with his long, lean frame gets in beside me, it feels much smaller.

Is he on my side? I think he might be.

I glance over at him as he shifts into place, and I shouldn't have done that because now I can both see *and* smell him and how the hell am I supposed to sleep in the same bed as him without *doing something* about it?

I draw in a deep breath. Another mistake since I'm simply drawing in Jack Dalton.

He stretches his legs out in front of him and sits up against the headboard, leaning on a pillow the same way I am. He bumps his knee against mine, and he leaves his there.

"Did you have a good night?" I ask softly.

"Oh, Katie," he says, and his voice is low and deep and raspy and *fuck* if it doesn't press directly on that ache already throbbing low down in my belly. Something about that nickname for me out of his mouth simply overwhelms me. "It was fine, but I know a way we can make it memorable." His voice is husky and dripping with sex, and I know if I glance over at him, his eyes will be smoldering at me.

My cheeks turn red. As much as I want exactly what he's offering—whatever it is—*memorable* doesn't mean it's a good idea.

So instead of answering, instead of looking over at him, instead of tempting him, instead of giving into whatever I think I might be feeling, I set my phone down, flick off my bedside lamp, turn away from him, and pull the covers over me. And then I whisper quietly, "Good night, Jack."

CHAPTER 25

I smooth down the front of my dress and stare at myself in the mirror a beat.

I should change.

It's too short, too tight, too low cut, too...everything I shouldn't be wearing tonight with someone I can't seem to stop lusting after even though he purposely pushes every single one of my buttons.

But it's what I picked out for my best friend's bachelorette party months ago, and tonight's the night, and somehow Jack is coming with me even though this is the worst idea in the history of bad ideas after we just got back from Los Angeles last night.

I won't be able to drink since I'm supposed to be the responsible one, and everybody at the table will censor themselves in front of the football superstar.

And I guarantee by the end of the night everyone in our group will know I'm the face behind the viral cat burglar meme because that's just the kind of thing Jack would do to further mortify me.

Nerves play in my chest, but I have to act like they don't.

I'm not nervous for the party.

I'm nervous to spend this sort of time around Jack. I'm nervous about what *he* might do.

My heart races and my tummy does a little flip when I make my way down to the kitchen and spot him already there waiting for me. He's wearing jeans and a black t-shirt, and he's standing by the sink staring out the window into the backyard.

His arms are folded over his chest and he leans casually against the counter. I glance at the biceps stretching the fabric of his shirt.

He is so freaking hot.

I study his profile for a beat—the shadow of scruff of his strong jawline, the sharp cheekbones, the straight nose, the full lips that already know how to work against mine.

God, I want to kiss him again.

I ignore the twinge between my thighs, and then he turns to look at me.

His eyes flick to my chest. "Nice dress," he says, playing it off like he was checking out the *dress* when the heat in his eyes tells the story that he was checking out the body beneath it.

"Thanks." The single word comes out all hoarse and raspy, and I clear my throat. "Shall we?"

He raises a brow. "Shall we...what?" His voice drips of sex, and I remind myself that this man is engaged to another woman.

It doesn't matter *why* he's engaged, and it doesn't matter if he *wants* to be engaged. He is, and that makes him off-limits.

I glance toward the hallway that leads out to the garage. "Leave?"

"We shall." We start walking toward the garage. Since I already determined I'm not drinking tonight, I volunteered to drive. No sense letting him drive and risking my life in his giant truck on the way to my bestie's bachelorette party.

We head toward Caesar's Palace because the bride wanted to party on the Strip. We booked VIP bottle service at a nightclub, so that means we have a table to sit at when our feet hurt from dancing, our club cover charge is paid for, and we have a waitress to keep the drinks flowing all night.

Which is great for everyone except me.

I've already paid my share—a cool three hundred fifty bucks to cover my own fun along with a portion of the bride's...and now I'll have to add a little more to cover my companion.

I pull into valet and drop my car, and we get out and walk toward the hotel entrance.

Jack is stopped immediately. He signs an autograph.

And another.

And another.

A group of people makes a circle around him, and we're not even in the doors yet.

He takes selfies. He shakes hands. He hugs fans. And he smiles through it all...but it's as I study him that I see a little something else through the smile.

He doesn't want to be here.

Not *here* here...I think he's fine with attending this party with me, maybe even a little curious about it, but there's something in his eyes that tells me he's doing this thing with his fans because he *has* to, not because he *wants* to.

What must that life be like? I'm getting sort of an inside look at it now, I suppose. We went to that restaurant with his family, where we were left alone in a back booth. We've been out and about over the last two weeks, but he's never been mobbed like this.

Those other times, though, he wore a baseball cap or sunglasses. He did things that seemed to be just enough to keep the attention off him like the expert he's likely become through years of experience. He did things that made people look over at him with curiosity or with that familiar question in their eyes as they wondered whether that was *really* Jack Dalton or maybe just someone who *looks* like Jack Dalton.

Tonight, that's not the case.

And something about that fact makes me really sad for him. He's this big, tough guy, so strong and controlled and disciplined, and he's been in the business long enough to know this is his life. But this is the first time I've actually seen this sort of thing firsthand.

The psychologist in me wants to analyze the situation. Does he want to escape because he doesn't like the attention?

From everything I know about him, he *loves* attention. He loves the spotlight. He loves his fans.

Is it because he's not happy about being traded to the Aces?

That could be it.

Is it because he's here with me?

His eyes meet mine as he poses for one more selfie. *Sorry*, he mouths.

My chest tightens as I realize that's exactly what it is. He feels bad that this is happening, that the attention is centered on him when he came here to do something for me.

I'm at once shocked and warmed. He's not exactly been the nicest to me, but somehow this feels like a breakthrough...like we've turned a corner and could almost be something resembling friends.

Even now that I think about it, I realize the fact that he even agreed to come here tonight with me puts us solidly on friendly terms. I'm not quite sure *why* he agreed to it, but here we are.

He escapes the mob of fans thanks in large part to one of the valet drivers who helps clear the crowd before he escorts us to our destination, and it's as we're making our way to the club that I glance up at him. His eyes are down on me, and I look quickly away.

I have to.

I can't be held responsible for my actions when someone as hot as Jack Dalton looks at me the way he just did.

"Thanks for understanding back there," he says, his voice low.

"What choice did I have?" I ask, going for modesty.

He shrugs. "Some women stand back and let me work. Some women try to take their place in the spotlight. Thank you for being the former."

He doesn't have to say that Michelle is the latter. It's clearly evident in his tone.

We're led back to our VIP table, where Shannon and the rest of the bridesmaids are already midway through their first drinks of the night.

"Holy shit, it really is Jack Dalton," Shannon says loudly enough so everyone at our table can hear her over the music. She stares at him in awe.

He offers her his signature lady killer smile. "It really is. Which one of you is the bride?" Shannon raises her hand, and his smile widens. Good Lord he's handsome. I'm ready to drop my panties right here.

Until he says his next words. "Kate slipped me a hundred to give you a lap dance later. I told her I would've done it for twenty."

"Wha—oh my God! What?!" I screech, and everyone around the table laughs.

Yeah, yeah. Ha freaking ha. He's teasing me again, and I guess I need to lighten up a little, but I'm not in the mood for his antics.

Shannon introduces the five ladies in the bridal party, starting with her sister, Sara. Everyone here is local to Vegas, which is fairly unusual as far as Vegas bachelorette parties run, and everyone is in awe that Jack Dalton is really here at their little party.

"Let's have some fun, ladies!" he says, and he's met with cheers and whoops from around the table from everyone except me. I fold my arms over my chest and sulk as I sink back into my chair while the others hold up their glasses in a toast. Jack looks at me and raises a brow, and then he picks up a glass, fills it with vodka, and hands it to me. He lowers his mouth a little closer to my ear. "Come on, Katie Cat," he says, and his warm breath tickles my ear. "That includes you."

"I can't drink," I point out. "I drove, and I'm responsible for you."

"I'll behave myself. Your best friend only gets married once. Just for tonight, let's reverse roles and I'll babysit you. I can drive us home, or worst-case scenario, we take an Uber."

I narrow my eyes at him as I try to get a good read on him. My gut tells me not to trust him, but I really want to just let loose and have a little fun. He seems sincere enough, and what harm could there be in one or two little drinks? I don't have to get *wasted* just because I have one or two. And it's bottle service. We paid an arm and a leg for this table, so I'd at least like to get a little something for my money.

I take the glass from his hand and hold it up as everyone at the table whoops and cheers again. "To the bride!" I yell, and I'm met with a chorus of "*To the bride!*" before we all toss back some vodka.

It burns going down. I haven't had straight vodka in a long time.

After the first few sips, it starts to go down a little more smoothly. We move to the dance floor a while, and Jack flirts with all the bridesmaids while he dances. He flirts with people *not* part of our party, too.

And I don't like it. I move in front of him to get his attention, and he dances with me a little. It's keeping him away from other people, which will keep him out of headlines.

That's what I tell myself, anyway. That's my big line of defense...that I'm just doing my job.

He keeps his hands to himself, but I want them on me. I want him to pull me in closer. I want to be close enough to smell like him when the night's over.

He turns to dance with Lauren, one of Shannon's other bridesmaids.

I drink a little more vodka to make that little twinge of jealousy disappear. It doesn't.

He dances with Sara a bit, and that twinge just seems to grow stronger. I fill my empty glass and drink a little more.

I get in front of him so he's dancing with me again. Liquid courage fuels me to grab his hand and set it on my hip. I keep my hand over his, and when his eyes meet mine in the flashing lights, a whole lot of heat passes between us as I think back to what happened the last time we had a few drinks in a nightclub together.

He's engaged.

He doesn't move his hand.

We had sex a few months ago and *I can't stop thinking about it.* Big, rough hands on my skin. His tongue brushing against mine. His eyes hot on mine as he moved inside me.

My chest tightens and a fierce ache presses between my thighs.

His other hand moves to my other hip.

His girlfriend showed up that night. The same girl who had his baby. The one he's engaged to now.

He doesn't love her.

She doesn't love him.

His hands feel so freaking good on my body again.

I drink a little more.

He leans down and nuzzles my neck, and butterflies dance around my belly and tingles zip down my spine as the scruff outlining his jaw tickles my skin.

I'm drunk enough that this seems like a good idea. I want to feel that scruff on my thighs as he dives face first into pleasuring me.

I lean into him and take in his scent, hot danger mixed with manly wood and a little gin. It's risky, but I have to breathe it in. I *have* to. My tongue darts out to get just the tiniest taste of his skin.

God, he tastes good.

The ache between my thighs pulses with need and my stomach somersaults.

I hold onto his neck with one arm as we dance, our bodies finding a rhythm on the dance floor as easily as they did on that couch last Halloween.

I tip back a little more vodka.

His eyes are on mine as we dance, our bodies shifting a little closer to each other as his fingertips dig into my hips.

He stares me down, and his eyes flick to my lips. I snag the bottom one between my teeth, and he blinks once as his eyes move back to mine.

The ache between my legs intensifies.

I want this. I want *him*.

But reality plows into me.

We can't do this.

It doesn't matter how much I want it.

He's engaged, and he has a kid, and I'm working with him...and it's all so very messed up.

I force myself to back away. It's the hardest thing I've ever done in my life, but someone has to be the strong one here. We can't take another step in the direction we're walking without major consequences for us both. Add that to the fact that we're both drinking, and there's nothing right about this situation except for how good he feels so close to me.

I head back to our table, and when I glance back, he's standing in the middle of the dance floor staring after me. We're each surrounded by the crush of partiers at a nightclub, yet we're two people who are very much alone.

I drown my good decision in vodka at the table by myself.

Shannon swings by to check on me. "I'm fine," I yell over the music, and she tries to get me back on the dance floor. "I need a minute," I say.

I drink a little more.

And then my responsibilities seem to fly out the window completely...right along with my consciousness.

I'm not quite sure what happens next, but it's very quiet as my phone pings with a notification. I should open my eyes to check that, but it's like they're glued shut.

It starts ringing. I feel around on my nightstand without opening my eyes, and I click it off to ignore the call.

Why did I possibly think that screeching ring tone was a good idea?

It starts ringing again, and each high note is like a sledgehammer to my skull. I ignore the call again.

When it pings with another notification, I lift my head.

That's my first mistake. I lie my head back down. I'm not getting out of bed today. Possibly never again.

My phone rings for the third time—at least the third time since I've been awake—and that's when the bed shifts beside me.

"Turn that fucking thing off," a deep, *familiar* voice beside me says, and my eyes pop wide open.

I sit up in bed and turn my head slowly to see whether Jack Dalton is really in my bed beside me, and sure enough...there he is.

He's tossed the covers off, and he lies there in a pair of shorts. That's it. Jack Dalton is lying in my bed wearing shorts and abs that are cut so gorgeously that I can see each and every ridge in the too-bright light of morning. He's not even flexing.

All I need to do is reach my hand over a few inches and I'd be able to feel every edge of muscle beneath his smooth skin.

Seriously, who has a body like that? Holy guacamole.

I blink my eyes a few times because surely this is a dream...or a nightmare. I haven't quite decided yet.

My phone starts ringing again, and I click it off before I finally look at the screen.

Twelve missed calls, and they're all from Calvin Bennett.

My heart races as I turn to look at the other side of my bed again. Jack's still lying there, but now there's a smirk on his face.

What the hell happened last night?

To be continued in Book 2, **TACKLED**.

ACKNOWLEDGMENTS

Thank you to my husband, my kids, my family, and my friends. Thank you to my editor (Trenda London), my beta readers (Diane Holtry, B. Roscoe, and Alissa Riker), and my proofreader (Becky Claxon). Thank you to Najla Qamber for the gorgeous cover design. Thank you to Dani Sanchez and Wildfire Marketing Solutions. Thank you to my ARC team, Team LS, and the members of the Vegas Aces Spoiler Room. Thank you to the bloggers who helped promote this series either through reviews or promotional posts. Thank you to my readers.

I'll save my longer acknowledgments for the final book since I know you're ready to get to the next book… and I can't wait for you to see what's next.

xoxo,
Lisa Suzanne

ABOUT THE AUTHOR

Lisa Suzanne is a romance author who resides in Arizona with her husband and two kids. She's a former high school English teacher and college composition instructor. When she's not cuddling or chasing her kids, she can be found working on her latest book or watching reruns of *Friends.*

ALSO BY LISA SUZANNE

HOME GAME
Vegas Aces Book One
#1 Bestselling Sports Romance

A LITTLE LIKE DESTINY
A Little Like Destiny Book One
#1 Bestselling Rock Star Romance

Made in the USA
Columbia, SC
22 February 2025

54230767R00114